A Tu

Avijit Sarkar

A Turn of Events

& other stories

To the four gorgeous and inspiring women in my life:
my wife Palu, my daughter Annie,
and my two beautiful granddaughters Olivia and Chloe

A Turn of Events & other stories
ISBN 978 1 76041 263 0

First published 2016 by
GINNINDERRA PRESS
PO Box 3461 Port Adelaide 5015
www.ginninderrapress.com.au

Contents

Introduction

Since the day I met Avijit in 1977, I realised that he was a little different from others. He was born to be a 'creative' and his extraordinary skills cover an astounding range of subjects from the creative arts to mathematics. However, since the day I married him, I have always admired his 'human' side – his love for cooking, his passion for travelling, his enthusiasm for shopping, his tongue-in-cheek sense of humour, his generosity and his untiring work in recent years to raise money for cancer research in Australia.

The collection of short stories in this book is a testament to his abilities as a keen observer of social structures within the Indian community in Australia and his illustrations in the book demonstrate his eye for characterisation and for detail. He is probably one of the most recognisable faces in the Australian-Indian entertainment industry but I am sure that his book will also establish him as an excellent raconteur and a writer par excellence. I hope that he writes many more such engrossing books.

During his lifetime, Avijit has inspired many people with his virtuosic abilities but I think that his greatest achievement – away from the limelight – has been his inspiration for me and the family, as a loving husband, a doting father, a funny grandpa.

Palu

My father, who was born in Calcutta in the 1950s, was raised in a traditional Hindu Bengali family. His parents were accomplished musicians but his upbringing was far from privileged. By the age of nineteen, he was doing musical performances to support his family, some days not able to have a meal himself. It was at that point in his life when he started to see the world differently. He started to disagree with many cultural norms and realised that many of the traditional values taught to him were outdated and irrelevant. So he started writing. His stories inspire an awakening of a society that has, for so long, lived in the dark and followed ancient ideals that no longer make sense.

This collection of stories is a true depiction of the way my father's mind works. He is no dreamer; he is a realist through and through. As a father, he taught me to question the world as I see it and to not succumb to the pressures of other people's thoughts and ideas. He encouraged me to look at the world, not through rose-coloured glasses, but with a cynical eye and to see the absurdity and hilarity in everyday things, and that's exactly how his stories have been written.

George R.R. Martin once wrote, 'A reader lives a thousand lives before he dies. The man who never reads lives only one.' In this book, you will live the lives of many intriguing characters and you will feel the full spectrum of emotions from anguish to surprise through to pure joy. Couple that with my father's satirical views of the world, and you have a truly entertaining read.

Annie

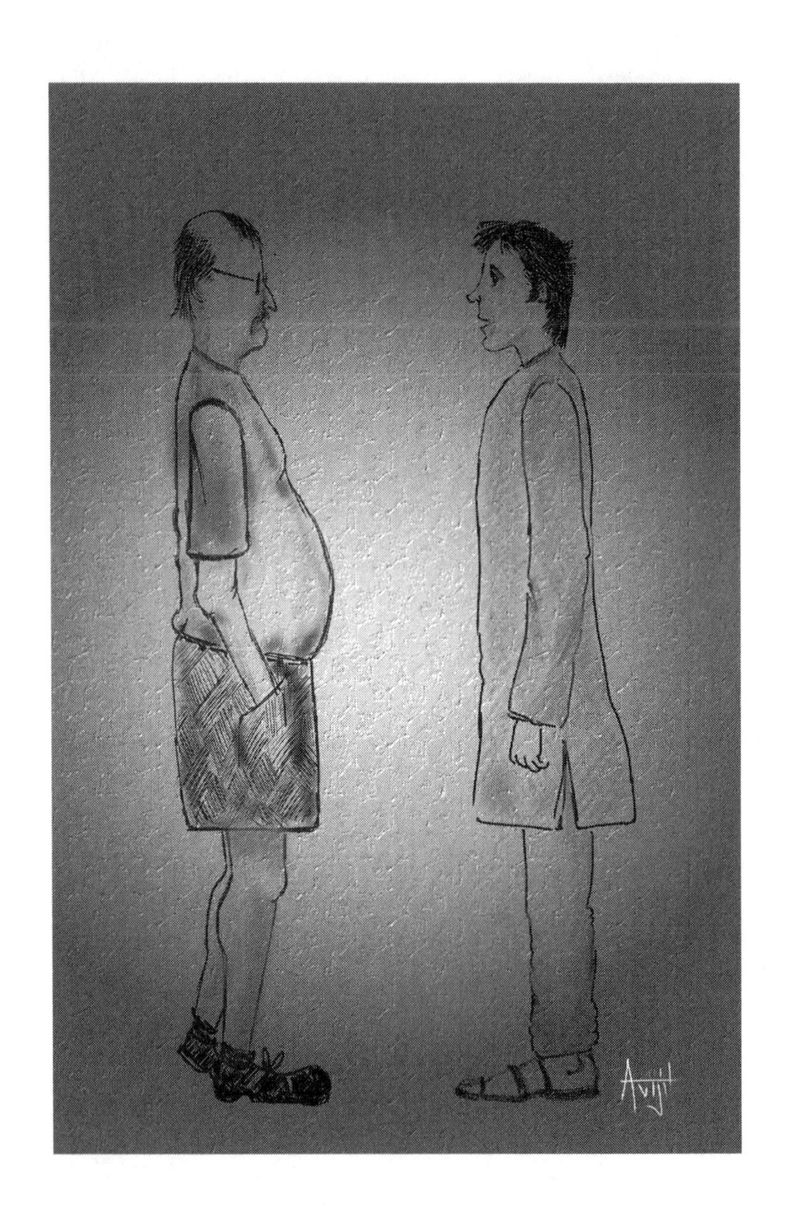
Avijit

A Turn of Events

I first saw Bipin Patel at my wife's medical practice. The year was 1990 and, having retired from active work, I had wholeheartedly immersed myself into my new duties, managing the front desk at the practice. What added to my interest in my new role was the ability to be a curious fly on the wall and study the sea of humanity that passed through the practice every day.

Bipin was a thin young man with an extremely poor taste in fashion. He also had a particularly uninteresting personality and his only remarkable (for want of a better word) feature was a very large mole under his right eye. He could hardly converse in English and I remember that I had to revert to the Gujarati language in order to communicate with him when he showed up for an appointment with my wife on that day. He had come in with a bad bout of flu but was asked to wait since there was an unusually long waiting list at the surgery. After looking aimlessly at the television for a while, he started up a conversation with an elderly Gujarati gentleman sitting next to him. From the bits and pieces that I overheard, I surmised that Bipin was going through hard times in Sydney and the strict government legislations on work practices for students hardly allowed him to make two ends meet.

After his consultation, as he came up to the desk to pay for the visit, my curiosity got the better of me. 'I overheard a fair bit of the conversation that you were having with the other gentleman,' I said. 'I hope you settle in well.'

Bipin was obviously thirsting for eager ears because he immediately let me into his complete family history, his current state of affairs and his plans for the future.

He had arrived in Sydney a year ago on a student's visa. Born on the outskirts of a small town called Nadiad in India, Bipin was raised in a lower-middle-class household. Like many others in the smaller towns in India, Bipin grew up amidst wanton hardship, unending yearnings and incurable impoverishment. Driven by sheer need and ambition, Bipin's father had educated him at the local college and then sent him to Australia to further his education. The downside was that, in order to get admission in a small dodgy college in the backstreets of Sydney, Bipin's father had to sell off his house and take a loan as well. All Bipin now wanted was to work in Sydney, pay off his father's loan, educate himself and then go back to his hometown with some extra money in his pockets.

I felt that his continuing struggle with the English language was only second to his struggle with life in Australia. His wife, who had travelled to Australia with him, was unemployed and hence he had to work long hours in three different jobs in order to run his household. His wife, I was told by him, was continuously looking for work but to no avail. In spite of all this, Bipin was excited because he had heard that the Australian government was about to open the doors for students to apply for permanent residency. However, when I spoke to him about his plans for the future, I was quite taken aback with his undying passion for India and his great dream of going back home to the small town in Gujarat with all the money that he would save in Australia.

Our next encounter was about a year later, once again at the surgery. I remember the day because there was an uncharacteristic heavy downpour in Sydney. I was immersed in some administrative work and I looked up as a shadow fell across the desk. It was Bipin and he had a very broad smile on his face. He had two pieces of news for me. One was that he had successfully acquired permanent residency in Australia and had already applied for his wife's permanent residency permit. The other piece of news was even more exciting: they now had a baby boy. When I asked him about his plans for the family, he was quick to reply that he wanted to get his permanent residency and then his citizenship for Australia only because he wanted his child to be an Australian citizen. He was, in fact, vociferously adamant about his child settling down in Australia and becoming what he termed as a 'real' Aussie. However, Bipin's own future plans had not changed. He still wanted to go back to his beloved homeland and settle there with his friends and family.

I saw him again after a span of probably nearly five years with his wife and his son, who must have been about four years old. This time, I was quick to observe that Bipin had a distinct change in his attitude. It was quite evident that while he spoke to his coy wife and to others with a heavy guttural Indian accent, he spoke very differently to his son. This change in his demeanour was subtle but quite amazing. He constantly addressed his son with an assumed accent which seemed to be his best imitation of the Australian vernacular. This was his 'real' Aussie accent. Phrases like 'Good on you, mate' and 'Fair dinkum' poured out in abandon. What was even more remarkable was the fact that the child had a surprising Australian accent and was being addressed by his parents as Bob! It was very obvious that Bipin was trying to pin the essential Australian personality on the child. When I spoke to him about my observations, Bipin had, as always, a very simple explanation. He did not want his son to be the typical Indian.

'We were born in India,' he said, 'and we cannot be anything else but true Indians. However, Bob needs to be a true Australian. He needs to talk like one, behave like one and live life the Australian way. I have made changes to my plans. Once Bob has settled down here after his studies, we will pack up and leave for good. Our town and our friends are still beckoning to us from India.'

That was the last time I saw Bipin at the surgery and, with the passing years, memories of him faded away.

It was only by chance that I came upon him a year ago at the local shopping centre. As I was transferring the contents of my shopping trolley into the boot of my car, I saw a car turn into the vacant spot next to mine. I looked up casually and I would not have known that it was Bipin Patel at the wheel, save for the trademark mole under his eye. As he stepped out of his car, he looked across at me and his face lit up when he recognised me.

It was twenty years since my first encounter with him and the changes were quite dramatic. His sense of fashion was leaning towards the more avant-garde and his Australian accent was shockingly pronounced when he spoke to me. 'How are ya?' he asked in what I thought was a distinctly nasal tone. 'Been a while now. Would be over twenty years, I reckon.'

I gulped and was a little slow in my response as I tried to fathom the change in the man's personality.

'Don't you remember me?' he asked, shutting the door of his Holden Commodore with a flourish. 'I'm Bipin Patel. I used to come to your wife's surgery. Gee! It's been ages, I say.'

I smiled back. 'Of course I remember you.'

We broke out into small talk about his family and life in Australia.

After a while, I could not hold back on my curiosity any longer. 'You've changed a lot, Bipin,' I said. 'Your English accent, the way you dress. You're so different now.'

Bipin looked at me with a gleam in his eyes. 'We decided to stay back permanently and shape our future in Australia,' he said proudly. 'It's a great country and we wanted to be a part of this place. Be an Australian in every way possible.'

'So,' I remarked, 'after all, you did change your plans of moving back to India.'

'Yes,' replied Bipin with a faraway look in his eyes. 'Opinions and beliefs change with time, I reckon. After twenty years in Australia, I felt like an alien during my last visit to India. These are different times. Things have changed in India and so have the people and their priorities.'

'Well, that's life, I guess,' I replied. 'And what about your son? If you've changed so much, I suspect your son would now be a true blue Aussie!'

Bipin stared at me for a few moments. When he spoke, he had a remote look in his eyes. 'There has been a strange turn of events in our lives,' he said. 'We tried to instil true Australian values and the Australian lifestyle in him. But Bob could never adjust to life here and was always keen on the Indian way of life. Last year, during our trip to India, he fell in love with that country. In fact, he also fell in love with a girl in our hometown. Since then, Bob has married and moved to India for good.'

A Marriage of Inconvenience

2009

Neelam Kaur was one of six prospective brides-to-be lined up for Gulshan Singh, as is often the custom in India for arranged marriages, especially in rural towns. Her father was approached by a friend about 'a very promising young Punjabi man' by the name of Gulshan who had landed from Australia, looking to get married. He was told that this young man had migrated to Australia on a student visa in 2007 and, after getting an accounting degree, he had managed to procure permanent residency. Young men like Gulshan, who carry a permanent residency from a developed nation, also carry a higher value in the wedding market in India, where parents constantly sniff around for a prospective candidate from overseas.

When Neelam's father spoke to her about the proposed liaison, she enacted the role of the coy young girl to perfection, as was often expected from young marriageable girls in conservative families. However, the joy within her heart was boundless. The prospect of marrying someone from Australia was a like a dream come true. After the conversation with her father, she rushed to the local village temple and offered her sincere prayers to the deity for this amazing opportunity. She even made a silent promise to donate ten rupees to the temple if she was selected by the groom-to-be.

A few days later, Neelam's father heralded the exciting news to the family. Gulshan was very keen to see Neelam. And true to his word, two days later, Gulshan paid a visit to Neelam's home accompanied by a group of close friends and family members. As was the tradition, the parents first had a discussion in private about the proposed alliance followed by a meeting between the prospective couple. A show of unspoken discretion was called for and the members of both families stepped outside into the little backyard, allowing some much-needed privacy for the young couple.

The evening ended with a lavish dinner that had been specially organised for the visitors. Gulshan's entourage left promising a reply by the very next day. Neelam spent a restless night, unable to sleep, while her parents, in the adjacent room, tossed and turned relentlessly through the night. As one might expect, prayers were in abundance throughout the household.

The good tidings arrived the next day, by way of a quick phone call from Gulshan's father. Neelam was the chosen one; Gulshan had been more than impressed with her looks, demeanour and attitude. What went unnoticed was the fact that it was actually the promised dowry that had done the trick. Of course, Neelam's joy knew no bounds. Her prayers seem to have been answered.

Since Gulshan was to leave for Australia within three weeks, the wedding date was decided quickly and the planning was done in great haste amidst a sense of urgency. Within two weeks, the couple was married off, lest the groom changed his mind at the last moment, as was sometimes the case in such alliances. The wedding, however, was a very joyous occasion for both families and no cost was spared for the festivities and in the care of the guests.

A few days after the celebrations, Gulshan took Neelam to the Australian embassy in New Delhi and applied for her immigration to Australia. A week after that, Gulshan left for Australia, leaving behind a new bride with fresh hopes in her heart and a sense of happiness in her soul. However, amidst these hectic events, Neelam did not get the opportunity to know her husband well. Had she done that, she might have had some inkling about his darker side.

Gulshan Singh had been raised in a family riddled with a history of domestic violence. The physical and mental abuse inflicted on the family by his father was the order of the day. As with many other things in life in India, Gulshan's family had just accepted the state of affairs and he had grown up seeing the frequent and violent physical abuse meted out to his mother. By the time he was in his teens, to the dismay of his mother, he started manifesting a vile temper not dissimilar to his father's. Gulshan's unpleasant temper was never quelled at home and, as men often do, he stepped into adulthood with the presumption that it was perfectly okay for males to be abusive and violent towards women.

Neelam's anguish started within a couple of months of her landing in Sydney and it was triggered over a very trivial matter. It was a Friday evening and Neelam had not been able to cook dinner due to an attack of migraine that she often suffered from time to time. Gulshan had come back late from work, completely exhausted and ravenously hungry, only to find that there was no food laid out for him. Within moments, he was in the bedroom in a manic rage. He hauled Neelam into the living room and demanded an explanation. Unable to understand the sudden rage, Neelam had retaliated with a slight show of her own temper. After that, it was utter pandemonium as she was beaten up mercilessly.

After this incident, violent abuse from Gulshan was a regular occurrence and it came to the point when Neelam simply accepted her state of existence and forced herself to accept her husband's misdemeanours. She had no intention of confiding in her parents because she felt that her confession might cause them unbearable anguish. She also felt mortally scared of talking to her friends in the neighbourhood, since she was quite sure that word would reach Gulshan – a thought that put the fear of God in her. She ultimately found an easy way out. She just maintained a code of silence and did the best she could for her husband, appeasing his every need and even cajoling him with extra affection, food and care. However, contrary to her hopes, this did not stop Gulshan from going into regular bouts of uncontrollable fits of temper that inevitably ended with violent attacks on Neelam.

Within one year, Neelam had a baby daughter and that brought more complexities to her life. She had to start living life with a dual objective: that of keeping her husband happy and at the same time protecting her little girl from any of his outbursts. It got harder by the day, but she remained resilient and shed silent tears only when she was alone with her daughter, often telling the little girl about the tragedies in her life while the little one stared back at her, unable to understand a word.

2010

Things took a turn for the worse when Gulshan's brother Amarjeet arrived in Sydney on a student visa. From then on, it was a case of two against one because Amarjeet was equally prone to fits of severe unprovoked rage. While Neelam's life started getting out of control with the increase in the violent outbursts from both the brothers, many of her friends advised her to report the matter to the police. But she steadfastly refused to do so because, in her opinion, that was not the morally correct thing to do. She maintained that such things were not to be discussed socially.

As the months passed, Neelam's life spiralled into an unending nightmare. She thought it would never end and at one point even thought of taking her own life, but her affection for her little child kept her going.

This went on for a year until a fateful hot summer morning.

Gulshan had left for work and Amarjeet was in one of his usual foul moods. Moreover, his impending college examinations added to his gloom. As he sat at the dining table reading his course materials, he repeatedly cursed the baby girl, who was constantly crying in the bedroom.

After a while, unable to contain his exasperation, he thumped on the table and raised his voice. 'Neelam! Keep the girl quiet,' he shouted.

'I can't. She seems to have a touch of fever,' replied Neelam. 'Why don't you go to the library and study there instead?'

Neelam's reply was like a fuse that ignited Amarjeet's temper. He got up, slamming the chair against the wall behind him, and walked into the bedroom. He tugged Neelam by the hair out into the living room. As Neelam screamed out, he beat her unpityingly and finally hurled her against the wall. He then calmly picked up his books and walked out of the apartment, muttering profanities under his breath.

Neelam lay on the floor, wiping away the blood that was oozing out of a gash on the forehead. She did not bother getting up and just lay there in shock, as tears streamed down her face. She could hear the child crying in the bedroom, but could not force herself to get up. She just lay silently on the floor for a very long time listening to the clock ticking away on the wall. Finally, she managed to get up and slowly stagger into the bedroom. She made her way to the bed and wiped off the blood from her face with a rag. Then, hugging her child close to her, she fell into a peaceful slumber.

A loud knocking on the front door woke her up. She looked around the room and then glanced at the clock on the table next to the bed. She had slept for over an hour. She looked down at the little girl sleeping soundly next to her and patted her softly on the head. The knocking increased in volume accompanied by occasional thudding on the door.

A stentorian male voice called out, 'Please open the door. This is the police.'

Neelam hurried out to the front door and, after fumbling nervously with the lock, she opened it. There were two men standing outside in police uniform.

'Madam,' said the elder man, 'would you know a gentleman by the name of Amarjeet Singh?'

'Yes,' said Neelam, her voice hardly more than a whisper. 'He is my brother-in-law.'

'Just wanted to let you know that Mr Singh has been admitted to the hospital with severe injuries,' the sergeant continued.

'How?' Neelam stammered. 'Wha– What happened?'

The policeman looked at her in a kindly manner and dropped his voice. 'He was assaulted by a group of young boys while he was walking from here to the library. We found your address in his pocket.'

'But why? He hardly knows anyone here,' Neelam said.

'We think it was just a random attack,' the sergeant continued. 'I think you should get to Westmead hospital as soon as possible. His injuries are quite serious. We'll need to come back later to ask you some questions about him, if that's okay with you.'

Neelam was too stunned to reply. She nodded consent and then slowly closed the door. She then ran to the phone and called Gulshan to tell him about the incident and asked him to rush to the hospital.

The next few days were chaotic. Gulshan and Neelam were questioned repeatedly by the police and in the end it was deemed that Amarjeet had been assaulted by a group of Middle Eastern youths for reasons unknown, while he was walking to the library. The injuries were quite horrific: broken ribs, broken nose, and a fractured jaw. The police failed to apprehend the assailants and within a few days Amarjeet was brought home.

Strangely enough, things suddenly changed in Neelam's life. She was the only person at home who could look after Amarjeet, since Gulshan had a seven-day work schedule at the local pub. Without her support, Gulshan realised that Amarjeet's recovery would be extremely arduous. She also had to do the daily household chores and look after the baby as well. Although the acceptance was reluctant and silent, the brothers realised that Neelam was their sole saviour and without her, life would definitely come to a standstill for the entire household. Suddenly, Neelam found herself to be an asset for the brothers.

Neelam, by her very nature, was a kind-hearted person and she felt that it was her duty to help Amarjeet. After all, Amarjeet was her husband's brother and a part of her small family in Sydney. She started caring for Amarjeet as a matter of priority. She fed him, washed him and made him food with mild spices that he preferred. After a few weeks, when he was able to get up, she helped him to hobble around in the apartment and even assisted him for short walks on the street outside. There was never a day when she forgot to give him his prescribed medicines and there was hardly ever a moment when she showed her frustrations or an inability to help the injured man. In fact, helping him gave her a feeling of satisfaction and even elated her spirits, especially when she caught him looking at her with a look that can be best described as 'soaked in thankfulness'.

The incident also subdued Gulshan and gave Neelam a sense of relief from his outbursts. He hardly ever yelled at her and his demands seemed to diminish. She felt that he had possibly realised her true worth as a human being. He even bought her a new Indian outfit from the local shop and some cheap toys for the little girl. It was a long time coming and things looked happy within the household. And Neelam, after many years, felt a sense of belonging.

2011

The effervescence of peace permeated through the household only for a year before things came to a head with an unforeseen incident. It happened during a Sunday afternoon lunch. Gulshan was home (having been sacked from the pub) and the two brothers, together with the little girl, sat at the table while Neelam prepared hot aloo parathas in the kitchen. It was a warm day; one of those days when one feels constantly thirsty. While Amarjeet played with the baby, Gulshan just sat there scowling at nothing in particular. He had been in a foul mood since the time he was made redundant at the pub.

'Neelam, can you get me a glass of cold water?' Gulshan said in a loud voice.

Neelam came out wiping her hands and got him a glass of water from the fridge.

Gulshan took a sip and scowled. 'Cold water, I said,' he growled. 'This is not cold.'

Neelam looked at him. 'That's the coldest that we have in the fridge today,' she said.

'Don't answer back,' he snapped back.

Amarjeet interrupted, hoping to bring this to a peaceful end. '*Bhai*,' he said. 'It's OK. Just relax.'

Gulshan turned on Amarjeet. 'Just shut the fuck up,' he screamed. 'Keep out of this. It's none of your bloody business.'

Neelam felt the need to interject. 'Please don't talk to your brother like that,' she said. 'He has done nothing wrong.'

Gulshan stood up, shaking with rage. He walked up to Neelam and shoved her to the floor muttering profanities under his breath as the petrified little girl looked on. Neelam saw a look on his face that she had always dreaded. The twisted smile...the grimace... She had seen that many times before and she knew exactly what was coming. She closed her eyes tightly and waited for the worst, her breath coming in small gasps. Instead, she heard a loud thud and opened her eyes. She stared in disbelief at Amarjeet, who stood over Gulshan while the latter squirmed in pain on the floor. Unable to contain himself any more, Amarjeet had physically intervened and, with a single punch, had sent Gulshan sprawling to the floor. Amarjeet had a look on his face that was quite similar to the one that Gulshan had sported a few moments ago.

Gulshan tried to get up, but fell back when he saw the look of hatred in Amarjeet's eyes. He tried to shout at Amarjeet but what came out of his voice was just a limp croak. He just lay on the ground whimpering like a child.

Neelam filed for a divorce within two weeks, under the guidance of a few of Amarjeet's friends.

Present day

Neelam Kaur now lives in a little townhouse with her new husband, Amarjeet Singh. Amarjeet is still seeing a psychiatrist about some residual anger management issues. He has a permanent job at the local pub and Neelam works two days a week at the grocery store around the corner from home. Her little girl is growing up well and she is still being taught to address Amarjeet as her dad. Life is looking surprisingly bright for Neelam Kaur. In fact, it has never been better since she stepped onto the shores of Australia.

Avijit

The Holy Man

I have often wondered whether this is a tale worth recounting. After what seems to be an unending stream of deliberations, I have now decided to document this particular incident; an incident that can be best described as uncanny.

The episode took place around twenty years ago when I was a bachelor sharing a struggling life in Melbourne with three others who were more or less sailing in a boat similar to mine. Three of us had jobs that were not worth writing home about and the fourth person simply did not have a job and did not want one either. We allowed him to live with us because of his ability to share the rent and also allow us to partake of his good life. Oh yes, he had a great life. Born of wealthy parents, Ravi was a man of leisure – a true Indian Baboo down under. He always had enough cash in his pocket to share around and without him we would have simply scratched a meagre existence. The only downside was his acerbic tongue. But then, money buys forgiveness quicker than the eye can follow.

We shared an apartment in the suburb of Clayton which was very popular with migrants from India. My other two flatmates were Hari and Dilip, both junior officers in the tax office. Hari was an avid reader and spent most of his time frequenting second-hand bookshops. Dilip, on the other hand, was a very religious man. He was a strict vegetarian who shunned any discussions about meat or any other food that was outside his periphery of pious beliefs. He also loved spending his spare time at temples and at religious discourses.

Neither Hari nor Dilip had many ambitions in life and nor were their academic qualifications conducive to higher aspirations. I, on the other hand, worked during the day as a part-time schoolteacher and studied computer science at night. My preoccupation with visions of a greater and better life was getting to a stage where it bordered on the incurable. Life was quite uninteresting to say the least, save for the weekends, when we strove to have some fun. These 'fun' events included cooking a couple of good curries or going to the movies. All expenses paid by Ravi of course. In fact, when his mood leant towards greater generosity, Ravi would even buy us a few bottles of beer from the local bottle shop. Dilip, the only teetotaller, would spend these evenings snorting away in disgust while we partied as best as we could.

I remember that it was a particularly cold Saturday evening when we decided to get some takeaway food from a small seedy Indian restaurant around the corner. To our delight, Ravi had also promised that he would get six large bottles of beer for dinner. That was definitely a big treat for all of us. I might as well mention that Dilip, who had been acting very mysteriously during the last few days, had disappeared early in the morning with the promise that he would bring a special guest to dinner that evening.

Ravi brought the promised beer as the clock struck seven and, without much ado, we got stuck into the chilled brew. Within the next hour, we had polished off three large bottles and our soaring spirits were aptly accompanied by loud laughter and meaningless chatter about no subject in particular. Ravi, who was in a very generous mood that day, had ordered a big takeaway dinner that included five curries. Around eight o'clock, Ravi asked Hari to go and pick up the dinner from the restaurant. Just as Hari walked towards the front door, we heard the rattling chimes of the old doorbell.

We looked at each other and smiled quietly. Dilip was here with his mysterious guest.

As we trooped out into the long corridor, we stopped dead in our tracks when Hari opened the door. Dilip stood at the door with a wide benign smile on his face and next to him stood a short man in a turban. He seemed to be in his late forties and wore a long gown (more like a nun's habit) of a light yellow colour. The turban on his head was large and of the same hue. The expression on this man's face could be best described as a cross between serenity and placidity.

Dilip stepped in with his companion and then introduced us to the guest. 'This is Babaji,' he said, the reverence in his voice unmistakable.

Babaji looked at us and smiled benignly.

'He is a very holy man, my friends,' Dilip continued. 'He is visiting Melbourne for a week and I have had the good fortune of spending a great part of the last couple of days with him.'

That explained Dilip's inexplicable behaviour over the last few days.

As Hari ran out to grab dinner, we trooped back inside. The holy man took his place quietly on a rickety wooden chair at one end of the room, while Dilip sat on the floor near his feet. I felt a little awkward picking up my glass of beer in the presence of someone who exuded pure holiness. But Ravi was in his true element and, grabbing a bottle of unopened beer, he walked over to the holy man and offered to pour out a glass for him. Dilip went white in the face and nearly stood up in protest. The holy man, however, smiled sweetly at Ravi and courteously declined his offer.

The evening seemed to pass quickly through the mists of intoxication and most of our judgements about time and space seemed clouded. Topics came and went quickly and arguments were hurled around the room with astonishing fervour. Tempers flew and jokes were shared in a jovial manner. All in all, it was turning out to be a great evening. Amidst all this, the holy man sat quietly in the corner, the benign smile never leaving his face for a moment.

Once Hari came back with the packed dinner, we opened the boxes with great enthusiasm. However, our mysterious guest refused to partake of the dinner, saying that he already had his once-a-day meal in the afternoon. That did not abate our appetite and we got stuck into the food passionately. Dilip initially refused to eat but filled his plate after the holy man had smiled at him and nodded his head in consent.

The post-dinner chatter continued and then stopped abruptly when we realised that we had not ordered any dessert. We looked helplessly at each other and decided that we might as well skip dessert, given the late hour.

But Ravi, whose spirits were soaring by then, pushed his hands into his trouser pockets and brought out a wad of ten-dollar notes. 'Here,' he drawled at Hari. 'Go and grab something from the shop round the corner. It should still be open.'

'Shop around the corner' always implied the seedy Indian takeaway joint from where we usually ordered our meals. The shop also stocked a variety of Indian sweetmeats and confectioneries.

'I'm bloody tired,' whined Hari.

'I think Hari's quite right,' I joined in. 'It's late anyway.'

Ravi stood up unsteady on his feet. 'OK, guys,' he said. 'I'll go and get something myself.'

'Don't worry,' said a quiet voice from the corner.

The conversation in the room came to an abrupt halt as all eyes turned towards the holy man.

He sat there smiling away. 'What would you like, my friends?' he asked in a calm voice.

'Rasgullas, of course,' said Ravi. Ravi had a penchant for this particular variety of Indian sweetmeat.

The holy man nodded and then slowly closed his eyes. A few minutes passed and we thought he might have fallen asleep. Ravi opened his mouth to say something, but Dilip stopped him with a motion of his hand. For reasons unknown, none of us spoke. We simply stared at the holy man in a hush.

After what seemed to be hours, the holy man suddenly opened his eyes. It was so unanticipated that I could hear sharp intakes of breath in the room. He beamed at all of us and then took off his turban very slowly. Everything seemed to be happening in slow motion and we simply sat there transfixed. We could hear nothing except the chime of the clock as it struck eleven.

As he took off the turban, I heard Hari whistle while Ravi uttered a profanity under his breath. I simply stared incredulously at the holy man while Dilip chanted what sounded like a prayer or invocation.

Perched precariously on the bald head of the holy man was a transparent plastic bag full of rasgullas.

No one spoke and the air was pregnant with silence except for the heavy breathing all around.

The holy man then stood up slowly, took the plastic bag off his head and handed it over to Ravi. 'Here's your dessert,' he said in a soft voice. 'Hope you like it.'

'That was a neat trick,' snarled Ravi, snatching the bag from the holy man.

'Was it?' The holy man asked. 'Sometimes there is a thin line between fact and fiction, as is there between life and death.'

Ravi was too drunk to absorb philosophies of life. He simply laughed at the holy man, his face twisted in a sneer. 'Was that your miracle for the day, sir?' He asked. 'Was that the proof of your holiness?'

Dilip stood up and protested vehemently.

Ravi turned on him. 'Do you really believe in these tricksters, Dilip?' he asked. 'What do you want me to do? Applaud loudly for a pathetic magic trick? Or do you want me to pay him a few dollars for the little hoax? Is that why you brought him here?'

Dilip turned red in the face and for a moment I thought he was about to hit Ravi. I quickly stood up and stopped the argument from turning ugly, while Hari put his arm around Dilip and gently lowered him into a chair.

Amidst all this, the holy man stood in the corner, completely unperturbed. He coughed apologetically and said to no one in particular, 'At times, all that you see is only limited by the perception of the eye. Sometimes you need to look beyond the eye and see the wonders of the world.'

'Wonders of the world, eh?' Ravi was shrieking by then. 'Bloody charlatan.'

The holy man looked at Ravi and there was almost a look of pity in his twinkling eyes. He then turned around to Dilip and indicated that it was time for him to leave. He smiled brightly, brought together his palms in a big namaste and quietly left the room, followed closely by Dilip, who had a sort of hangdog look about him.

The room remained silent after their departure. Ravi still had the sneer of distrust on his face while Hari still looked shell-shocked. As for me, I simply did not know what to believe.

Next day, by the time I opened my eyes, it was past ten in the morning. I looked around and realised that my other three friends were still in deep slumber. The previous night's incident had left an unpleasant taste in my mouth. My head was still heavy as a result of the alcoholic residues of the night and the air was still thick with the stink of stale liquor and leftover food. I decided to take a stroll and grab a breath of fresh air.

After a quick shower, I left the apartment, closing the door softly behind me.

It was the usual quiet Sunday morning in the neighbourhood. I walked out of the apartment and headed towards the shops around the corner to grab a cup of tea at the Indian takeaway shop. As I entered the shop, Abdul, the proprietor of the shop, waved out to me. He always maintained an air of joviality at all hours of the day.

'How are you?' he asked.

I waved out cheerfully to him. I was too tired to enter into a conversation that morning. I just strolled over to one of the many tables near the window and ordered a cup of tea and some toast. There were hardly any customers at that time of the morning and Abdul soon walked over to my table with my breakfast.

'You guys seem to be keeping some very odd company these days,' he said.

'Odd company, did you say?' I frowned at him.

He nodded and smiled. 'Strange but very holy company,' he chuckled.

Curiosity got the better of me. 'What are you talking about, Abdul?'

'That strange man in the yellow robes and turban,' he said. 'Looked like an Indian fakir to me.'

I stared at Abdul. He must have seen him walking towards our apartment with Dilip. Then, on second thoughts, I decided to probe a little further. 'When did you see him?' I asked.

'Late last night,' Abdul mused. 'At around eleven, I think.'

I stared at Abdul shaking my head. 'It couldn't have been eleven because he left our place at around midnight.'

Abdul laughed loudly. 'You are mistaken, my friend. You must have been quite drunk, I bet,' he said with a laugh. 'The holy man came down here to my shop and purchased a bag of rasgollas for you guys. But he left in a bit of a hurry, though, as if he needed to rush back. Very strange, I thought.'

But I was not listening to Abdul any more. I felt a slight sweat break out on my forehead. I just sat there staring at the cup of tea for a long time. I seemed to have lost my appetite. I put some money on the table and quietly walked out of the shop, leaving behind the cup of tea and toast. I had also lost the desire for a casual walk.

A Judgement of Character

It was Groundhog Day for Raj Krishnan. The end of another tiring and long day at work. He could hardly keep his eyes open amidst the jostling throng in the crowded train compartment. It reminded him of the jam-packed trains at Mumbai during his university days. He looked around for a seat and caught a slight movement to his right. An elderly woman was gathering her belongings – a shabby cheap handbag and a couple of shopping bags – to get off at the next station.

Raj pushed firmly against the resisting horde and edged towards the woman. As he drew closer, the woman got up. Raj sighed loudly with relief and pleasure. From the corner of his eye, he saw a couple of women in the crowd eyeing the vacant seat. Raj made his move, letting formalities and etiquette take a back seat. He chucked his briefcase quickly on the vacant seat, took off his jacket and sank into the seat with a sigh.

Raj rubbed his eyes and leant back, spreading his legs under the seat in the front. He was having too many late nights at work...drinking too much beer in the evenings. He must stop drinking...especially on days like this. He had hardly eaten anything since his morning brunch. It was a bad day. He had an argument with his manager, misplaced some critical documents and then developed an irritating headache in the afternoon. He needed some much-needed sleep. He glanced at his wristwatch. He could have a full hour's nap before the train reached St Mary's station. He slumped back in the seat and closed his eyes.

After a few frustrating minutes, Raj opened his eyes and looked around the compartment. Since his early days at the university in Mumbai, Raj had nurtured a secret passion. He loved analysing characters around him; especially in crowded places. He would observe people's mannerisms, their clothes, movements and looks. He would then try to deduce their profession, character and other details. He fancied himself to be a Holmes-like personality and often prided himself on his deductions and observations. In the process, over the years, he had developed a keen eye for details and a sense of judgement of character. Or so he thought.

The pair of men who sat facing him, two rows away from his seat, caught his attention. Wanting to while away his time, Raj set his deductive skills in motion. He sat up in his seat, took the newspaper out of his briefcase and spread it out, holding it upright in front of his eyes. That gave him the perfect opportunity to study his subjects under the guise of reading the newspaper. He had often used this trick in the past on several occasions and had mastered the technique to the point of perfection.

Raj first turned his attention towards the man sitting on the left. He could hardly suppress a smile. He had seen quite a few of this type, especially on the railway platforms at inner-city stations. The subject was young. Raj estimated the age to be around thirty. Unshaven, long blond hair tied in a pigtail. Raj took a note of the nicotine-stained fingers with distaste and his disapproving gaze moved over the man's shabby T-shirt and torn jeans. After completing his observations, Raj organised his thoughts into a set of logical deductive processes about his subject. He decided to call him Bernie. Caucasian. Obviously, the guy did not have a decent job. No wristwatch and therefore no regard for time either. No spare money in the pocket and hence the torn jeans and old T-shirt. Definitely a smoker. And that vacant look in the eyes… Drugs? Absolutely no regard for personal looks or hygiene… Possibly on the dole too. That stagnant wooden expression…could be dangerous!

Raj shifted his eyes to the other man and felt amused. Here was a completely different personality. Raj took a deep breath and started his analysis. What a remarkable difference! The second subject was a middle-aged Indian man, possibly in his early fifties. Raj noted the refined clothes, the silver-rimmed glasses, clean nails and well combed hair. It all added up to a distinguished look. Raj narrowed his eyes as his deductive abilities went into top gear. He thought about a few names for his second subject and decided on Ram. Definitely an executive, possibly in a good organisation. Expensive suit. A lawyer? Accountant? Had the spare money to afford that suit... Good education and upbringing. That high forehead... a definitive indication of intelligence. Clean-shaven, neat hair and good poise. Rama the Indian god. Yes, the name suited the man perfectly. He was sweating a little, though.

Raj leant back and closed his eyes meditatively. Bernie and Ram. Raj could not help smiling to himself. Where would Bernie be heading? Possibly to a seedy nightclub near Penrith? Didn't look like he would have a family to go back to, at this time of the evening. Or perhaps he did have a family...a battered wife, neglected children housed in a shabby housing commission apartment that smelt of stale beer and cigarettes. Raj grimaced. He opened his eyes and looked again at Bernie's claw-like fingers. They reminded him of a bird of prey. Raj could not suppress an involuntary shudder.

He closed his eyes again and let his thoughts dwell on his next subject – Ram. Ram, on the other hand, would be going back to a well organised home and a loving family. A large house in an affluent suburb near Penrith perhaps...well-kept gardens, good furnishings. He would probably be welcomed back home by a well-groomed wife while his children would be busy on the computers or poring over their studies. Going by his age, he would probably have kids in university or in high school. By a stretch of his imagination, Raj could even imagine a well-mannered Labrador barking away in the backyard to welcome his master back home and the smell of dinner wafting through the house. He could almost smell the chicken curry and rice...

Raj opened his eyes with a start and looked outside. The train was whizzing past the Mount Druitt station. He needed to get off at St Mary's. Two more stops to go. He pushed his newspaper into the briefcase, picked up his jacket and walked unsteadily down the aisle, towards the exit. As he passed his subjects, he could not help taking a quick look at them. Bernie was gathering up a small plastic shopping bag; the wooden look still etched on his face. Ram was picking up his briefcase and getting up. Raj smiled to himself. What a strange coincidence. Both Bernie and Ram were getting down at St Mary's!

Raj got down gingerly, as the train came to a screeching halt. Once he got off the train, Raj immediately forgot about his subjects and focused on matters at hand. He wondered what kind of dinner he was going to cook for himself and cursed under his breath. There were no eggs left in the fridge. Fried eggs came in very handy when he was late from work. He frowned. He would have to do with some soup packets and toast. Sometimes he wished that he had a wife and family to go back to. He hurried along the platform and was on the main street within minutes. He paused for a while and then decided to take the shorter route home through a little backstreet. This route would take him straight to the little takeaway shop a few blocks away from his apartment. He could then buy some sandwiches for dinner.

Raj walked down the main thoroughfare in front of the station and then turned into a dark lane. He peered at his watch and cursed under his breath. It was getting late and he needed to hurry. The takeaway shop might close. As he quickened his steps, his mind raced over the altercation that he had with his manager. Raj felt the anger seeping through him. The son of a bitch. If this continued, he might as well look for another job. Raj let out a profanity under his breath. He hated job interviews.

Raj heard the sound of footsteps behind him and suddenly realised that he was not alone on the street. He looked back apprehensively over his shoulder and nearly let out a loud laugh. It was Ram – his subject from the train! What a surprise, he thought. He slowed down his pace so that Ram could catch up with him. He realised that this might be a unique opportunity to test his powers of deduction. He could easily start up a conversation with Ram and then corroborate all that he had deduced about him. Raj slowed down and was surprised that Ram had not still caught up with him. He stopped to look around and see where his subject was.

Ram hit him even before he had turned his head completely. The single powerful hit was delivered with the briefcase, to the side of the head. As he fell, Raj saw a little flash as Ram moved his right hand in a quick sideways motion, slashing him with a razor-like object. Raj collapsed to the ground silently and, as his head hit the concrete, he felt the blood dripping from his midriff. Then came the excruciating pain. He wanted to scream but could hardly utter a syllable as bile gushed into his mouth. Through the painful daze, he felt hands fumbling in his pocket as Ram removed his wallet. After a few moments of darkness, Raj felt a tug at his neck as the gold chain was torn away and then he felt the gold ring being pulled from his index finger. After that, Raj felt nothing, as the world around him dissolved into a pitch-black tunnel. He did not see Ram gloating at the loot in his hands and he did not see the assailant's hands shaking uncontrollably with drug-induced withdrawal symptoms. Raj's lifeless eyes just stared into the bloodshot eyes of his killer kneeling over him.

Ram got up with surprising agility from his kneeling position and ran back through the dark alley, heading back towards the station. He looked anxiously at his watch through the beads of perspiration that streamed down over his eyes. He cursed loudly. He had only a few minutes before the drug peddler at the station left for the day. He must get his hit tonight. If he missed his shot, he felt that he would have to go back to his lonely dilapidated house, put his head on the dirty pillow and die a slow death. Even in his disconcerted and confused state, he felt elated. The salary that he earned from his job had never been enough to support his drug habit. But now, he had enough loot in his pocket to buy drugs that could last him an entire month. An entire month! In fact, he might even have some leftover cash to buy another decent jacket and a good tie that he could use. Good clothes always worked miracles for him when he stood at the long queue at the welfare office or approached unsuspecting victims whom he robbed.

As he reached the main street, Ram raced furiously towards the railway station. He kept an eye on the ground to avoid tripping over. If he had looked up, he might have caught a glimpse of Bernie walking into the doorway of Western Melody studios, after a quick smoke outside the building. Smoking was banned inside the studio and Bernie had a long recording session ahead of him. Bernie, of course, was the principal sound engineer at this boutique recording studio, owned and operated by his wife. He was also one of the most respected and loved characters in the recording industry.

A Doctor in the Making

Anondo and Sumita Mohapatra were among the many Indian doctors who migrated to Australia in the early seventies; a part of the big influx of medical practitioners to Australia, who were given the vintage red carpet welcome. Since Anondo had some friends in Adelaide, the couple decided to settle in the city of churches and they were quite surprised when they were offered positions in several hospitals. They decided to accept positions at Royal Adelaide Hospital, where they worked for a few years before establishing their own private practice in North Adelaide.

For the next twenty years, Anondo and Sumita worked incessantly; six days of the week, nine a.m. to six p.m. It was also a harrowing time on the personal front since they also had two children, three years after they set foot into Australia. While the parents made sure that affluence was guaranteed for the future, the two children Kamal and Preeti grew up in a household where there was no dearth of comfort but a little lack of the closeness that is so common among ethnic families.

The years flew by and the children grew up into well-mannered and well-spoken individuals. By the time they finished the primary years at a local private school, Anondo decided that Sumita should start working part-time and focus on the children's studies. It was imperative that the children should be made to work hard so that they could focus on getting the grades needed to get into medical school. Sumita agreed wholeheartedly because they knew of no other profession that was as worthy as medicine. In fact, they hardly cared about other professions. For them, a career in medicine would be an assurance of lifelong affluence and, more importantly, a long-lasting social status. Nearly all their friends were doctors and most of the kids were either in medical school or being groomed to get into one. This was a favourite topic when the families got together for social lunches and dinners, and information about grades and selective subjects in school was exchanged with great alacrity and excitement. Most of them also shared a common disdain for other professions, except perhaps for legal studies. Financial affluence and social supremacy were the order of the day. Nothing else really mattered. It was, therefore, a natural consequence that the children imbibed much of the discussions that went on between parents and most of the kids were mentally tutored to accept that a future in medicine was assured.

Kamal and Preeti were both extremely bright kids and the goading from their mother only added to their success. They consistently topped their classes and were shining examples among their peers. Anondo and Sumita also never missed an opportunity to proudly showcase their children at social gatherings.

As the years flew by, Kamal got through his HSC examinations with exceptional success and was soon accepted in the School of Medicine at Flinders University. It was a moment of extreme joy and pride for the family that culminated with a big dinner for friends where Kamal was, of course, the centrepiece. It was a joyous occasion for everyone. Everyone except Preeti. Her joy was marred by a lurking trepidation for the future because Preeti had no interest in medicine whatsoever and had an inherent dislike for subjects that dwelt on anatomical and biological matters.

Preeti was as brilliant as her elder brother and even achieved better grades at school. However, the subject closest to her heart was mathematics and her sheer brilliance in this subject was a widely discussed topic among her school teachers. For some time, she had been nurturing a secret desire to do her future studies in mathematics and if possible, even dedicate her career to doing research in allied areas. However, she lived in dread of her parents and could hardly even muster up enough courage to discuss this matter with them because she knew the likely aftermath of such a conversation. She therefore decided to broach the topic with her parents closer to the time of her HSC examinations.

It was during the first term of her HSC year that Preeti decided to tread on the subject with her parents. It was a usual evening in the Mohapatro household. Her mother was in the kitchen getting dinner ready for the family and her father had just come back from the practice; tired and a little short-tempered as always. As the family gathered around the dining table and dinner was served, Preeti took a deep breath.

'I wanted your advice on a particular matter,' she said, looking at her parents.

Anondo looked at her with a smile and then glanced at Sumita, who shrugged, indicative of an 'I don't know what'.

'I know how you guys feel about our future and our careers,' Preeti continued. 'As children we've been fortunate to have had so much guidance and encouragement from the both of you.'

Anondo and Sumita had bright smiles on their faces.

'Of course. That's important for you,' Sumita said. 'What would you do without a proper career and a good profession?'

Preeti looked down and took a very long and deep breath. She was not enjoying this at all. She helped herself to some hot rice and the perennial fish curry. 'But medicine is not the only proper career, is it?' she asked. She felt a little breathless.

'What do you mean, Preeti?' Anondo asked. 'There might be many professions, but nothing comes close to medicine.'

'The money. The social status.' Sumita joined in and smiled at Preeti.

There was a short lull in the conversation.

'Money and status?' asked Preeti. 'Even at the cost of happiness?'

Anondo looked up sharply at her. The smile had been replaced by an ugly frown.

Preeti looked down at her plate. The dreaded moment had arrived. 'I was wondering if I could do something other than medicine,' she said. 'Something that might provide greater challenges to me and, above all, make me very happy.'

The atmosphere around the table tensed up. Anondo's mouth was agape as he scowled at Preeti. Sumita had a look of disbelief spread across her face as she stared at Anondo. By then Preeti had lost her appetite.

'Are you joking, Preeti?' Anondo asked in a choked voice. 'Happiness? What would you know about happiness?'

'Are you really contemplating pursuing another career instead of medicine?' Sumita asked. The pitch of her voice had gone up a few notches.

Preeti looked at Sumita. She could feel the sweat on her forehead. 'I do appreciate the nobility of the medical profession,' Preeti stammered. 'It's just that my interest lies elsewhere. I want to pursue another career.'

Anondo had stopped talking by then. His face had taken on a crimson hue as he choked over every morsel of food.

Sumita glared at Preeti. 'And what would that be, Preeti?'

Preeti sensed the slight trace of menace in her mother's voice. She looked away, unable to look into her mother's eyes. 'Well,' she said at last. 'My interest lies in mathematics.'

Preeti heard a sharp intake of breath as Anondo found his voice.

He leaned forward on the table and looked at Preeti, his face flushed. 'So what will you become? A bloody mathematics teacher?' he asked in a rasping voice.

Preeti gathered up the last vestiges of her courage and looked up at him. 'What's wrong with being a mathematics teacher?' she asked.

Anondo gulped and stood up.

'Dad,' Preeti said in a pleading voice. 'I do not want to be a teacher. Please listen to me. I want to do higher studies in mathematics and then apply for a research position in one of the leading universities of the world. Maybe Harvard or MIT. I know that I can do it, Dad. I know that I have the capacity to do it.'

'I don't want to listen to this bullshit any more,' Anondo said and turned away from the table. After a few hasty steps, he turned to Sumita. 'I want you to handle this, Sumita,' he said and made a dramatic exit.

Preeti felt helpless and lost. She looked at her mother and was surprised to see tears in Sumita's eyes. 'Mum,' she said extending her hand towards her mother.

'That's enough,' Sumita said. 'This is the most disappointing thing that I have heard in my life. All this…after all our struggles and all the sacrifices. How will I face my friends? What will your brother say?'

With those parting words, Sumita left the room leaving behind a girl who felt that she needed a helping and caring hand around her shoulder. She wished that she had someone who could understand her.

From that day onwards, Anondo refused to speak to Preeti and she often found her mother's eyes wet with tears. Anondo refused to sit down at the dinner table if Preeti was around and Sumita often complained about having sleepless nights. The environment gradually worsened and Preeti soon felt like a stranger in her own house. She really wished that her brother was around to comfort her. She was also acutely aware that she needed to do her very best at her HSC; but given the circumstances at home, she could hardly focus on her studies. She realised that in the pursuit of her own goals and ambitions, she had shattered the dreams and aspirations of her parents. She had caused grievous heartache to the very two persons whom she loved the most. The next three days were the most painful ones in her life and, on the fourth day, she took decisive action.

After her parents had retired for the night, Preeti walked up to their bedroom and knocked on the door. She could hear her father snoring. After a few bold knocks, she heard her mother get up.

'What is it, Preeti?' Sumita asked. The irritation in her voice was unmistakable.

'I need to talk to both of you,' Preeti replied.

Sumita replied after a pause. 'It's nearly midnight. Can't it wait till tomorrow?'

Preeti could hear her father's muffled voice by then. 'No,' she said firmly. 'We need to talk now.'

The door opened with a jerk. Sumita stood there. 'What's so important?'

Preeti did not reply and simply walked past her into the bedroom. Anondo was sitting up on the bed. Preeti saw the scowl on his face. That's a really distasteful look, she thought to herself.

'Sorry,' she said. 'I know it's very late. But you need to hear me out. Please.'

'OK, what is it? Some more career-enhancing decisions?' asked Anondo sarcastically.

This was the first time he had spoken to Preeti in the last three days and, in spite of the deteriorating situation, Preeti felt elated just listening to his voice. She realised how much she loved her father.

'Yes, Dad,' she said with a smile. 'This is indeed a career-enhancing decision because I have decided to try and get into medical school.'

For Anondo and Sumita, it seemed as if a celestial glow had descended from the heavens into the room. Their scowls were immediately replaced by glowing expressions and broad smiles.

Sumita could hardly restrain herself and gave a big hug to Preeti. 'That's my daughter,' she said, holding back tears of joy. 'I knew that common sense would prevail.'

Anondo looked on silently for a moment before speaking. 'You have made us very proud, Preeti. Very proud indeed. You have shown proper respect for our aspirations and ambitions. Well done. Now all that you need to do is to get down to your studies and prove your mettle.'

By the time Anondo finished his impromptu short speech, Preeti was already at the door. 'Good night,' she said as she walked out.

Her parents hardly noticed her sagging shoulders and the painful expression on her face.

Preeti was a girl with very strong determination and she soon put her head down among the books. Her final grades, as expected by the family, were exceptional. Her first choice was Flinders University where her brother Kamal was studying and when she was accepted at the university, she felt engulfed in happiness. For a few days, she even forgot the incidents of the past year.

However, the next five years proved to be the worst in Preeti's life. She forced herself to take a liking to the subjects as they came along and trudged through oceans of knowledge that covered everything that the study of medicine encompassed. She accepted the study of human anatomy and physiology, and slogged through the complexities of the cardiovascular, respiratory and renal structures, together with other complex subjects. The months and years passed by very painfully but she persevered. She needed to make her parents' dreams come true. They wanted a medical degree from her and she was determined to get one for them. During difficult moments, she would often remind herself that she loved her parents like none other and a medical degree was a small price to pay for their lifelong ambition, hard work and sacrifice. But she never ever lost track of mathematics and, unlike any other medical student, in her spare time she delved into mathematics journals and research papers. While the study of medicine was driven by Preeti's moral obligations, her indulgence in mathematics was a labour of passion borne out of her unfulfilled ambitions.

In the next five years, Sumita retired from medical practice and Anondo cut down his hours at work. He continued to work in the hope that one day his children would maintain and participate in his medical practice. His joys knew no bounds when Kamal decided to pursue general practice and joined him at work. His next few years were spent in grooming Kamal into the practice and he nurtured a secret hope that one day, his daughter would be able to do the same. He often discussed with Sumita about the possibility of converting their medical practice into a full-blown medical centre and would often stay awake at night thinking about it. It would set the children on a path of unbelievable success and they would be the envy of his friends.

Although they had full confidence in Preeti's abilities, their anxiety and apprehension increased as Preeti's final exams drew closer. Sumita even offered to take up temporary accommodation near Flinders University in order to provide moral support for her daughter. Preeti firmly but politely refused the offer. Once again, as expected, Preeti passed her medical exams with flying colours and the elation in the Mohapatro household reached new highs. This was the final feather in the caps of Anondo and Sumita; the final jewel in their social crown. They waited eagerly for Preeti to wind up at the university and come back home. After consulting with Kamal, they even decided to host a welcome home celebratory party for Preeti. However, when they informed Preeti about the planned event, they were rather surprised to see the lack of interest in Preeti's demeanour. In fact, they were surprised and even quite disheartened when Preeti informed them that she wanted to return home only after the graduation ceremony at the university. However, nothing could dampen the spirits in the Mohapatro household and, after a wait of nearly seven weeks, Anondo and Sumita flew over to attend the graduation ceremony at the university.

The ceremony was a grand affair and wonderfully organised. The only inhibiting factor was Preeti's attitude. She seemed constantly distracted and spoke very little with her parents. On the day of the ceremony, they had special photographs taken at the campus and the evening was dedicated to a dinner with friends in Melbourne, at a very expensive restaurant. During the dinner, Sumita looked across the table at her daughter and several times exchanged warm smiles. Yet Sumita felt that the warmth was quite distant and her daughter seemed preoccupied with her own thoughts. As a mother, Sumita knew that her daughter was not her usual self; there seemed to be something weighing on her mind.

Within a couple of weeks after their return from Melbourne, the Mohapatras hosted the big bash for friends and family. It was a huge event and bigger than any other that they had hosted. As planned, the party personified all that Anondo and Sumita stood for and it was a culmination of their joy, pride and ambitions. With both their kids having passed medical school, they immediately went up a few notches on the society ladder. Preeti was, of course, the showcase of the party and she was paraded around proudly by her parents. To her joy, Sumita also noted that Preeti was back to her usual courteous self as she went around indulging in small talk with the guests. Anondo was a dream host for the evening and spared no expenses in making his friends welcome into what he often referred to as the household of doctors.

The day after the event, Preeti left home quite early while her parents, overcome with the tiredness from the previous night, slept in. When they woke up, they were quite surprised to find that Preeti had gone out without informing them. This was not her usual behaviour. Anondo tried calling her a few times on her mobile phone but there was no response. After that, he got busy attending to congratulatory phone calls about Preeti's success.

Preeti returned home just as the table was being set for lunch. As she walked into the dining room, Anondo noticed that she carried a neatly wrapped package under her arm.

'Right on time,' he said with a smile. 'Lunch is being served.'

As Preeti pulled up a chair at the dining table, he also noticed unmistakable traces of excitement in her. Must be something to do with the package, he thought.

'Sumita,' he called out. 'Preeti is here now.'

'Great!' said Sumita as she came out of the kitchen, a steaming platter of chicken biryani in her hands. 'Here's my special treat for my daughter.'

Preeti looked at her, her eyes softening. 'I'm not having lunch, guys. I have some urgent matters to attend to,' she said.

Her parents looked disappointed.

'But before I leave, I need to show you something,' she said, placing the package on the table.

'Ah!' said Anondo. 'And what has my daughter brought today? A gift for us?'

'Yes, Dad,' replied Preeti with a twinkle in her eyes. 'The greatest gift of your lives.'

Anondo and Sumita hunched over the table as Preeti opened the package. They gasped with pleasure and surprise when they saw the contents. It was Preeti's graduation certificate framed in one of the most exquisite wooden frames that they had ever seen. The framed certificate looked stunning, like a beautiful piece of artwork.

'This is beautiful,' Sumita said. 'What a magnificent frame.'

'This is for you and Dad,' Preeti said, looking at her mother. 'I chose the frame so that it can be displayed at a spot in the house where every visitor can see it. This is the ultimate gift that underlines your lifelong ambition and objective.'

Anondo held the framed certificate in his hands as if it was a priceless painting. Lost in joyous thoughts, he hardly listened to what Preeti was saying. He looked up with a start as he felt Preeti's hand on his shoulder.

'A few years ago, I made a promise to you on this dining table. I have now honoured that promise,' Preeti said.

'And we are proud of you for doing that,' Sumita said.

'My duty towards fulfilling your final ambition in life is now complete,' Preeti continued. 'I am sure that I have made you very happy.'

'Of course you have,' Anondo said in his usual authoritative voice.

Preeti looked away for a moment. 'As for me,' she said, in a voice that sounded softer than usual. 'I have now enrolled into the School of Mathematics at the Australian National University. Hopefully, I will be able to get an admission into Harvard or MIT in a few years.'

A veil of silence suddenly descended upon the room broken only by a few startled gasps from Anondo. Out of the corner of her eyes, Preeti saw her mother collapse into a chair.

Preeti continued. 'I have lived in your dreams till now. It's now time for me to follow my own. It's time to fulfil my ambitions…it's time for me to be happy.'

The room was pregnant with a suffocating silence as she got up from the dining table. Anondo had a look of incredulity etched on his face and Sumita looked on as if she had seen a ghost.

At the door, Preeti turned around and looked at her parents with a confidence that she had never felt before. 'And please don't wait for me,' she said. 'I'm having a celebratory dinner with my friends.'

Preeti then closed the door quietly behind her and walked into her own new world.

The Hand

The year was 2001. The rental market was heating up in the suburbs close to Sydney's CBD and Ramesh Kelkar was tired of looking for a place to rent in the inner city. He was in search of an apartment that he could share with his two mates, Luke and Marcello. Both his friends had reasonably good jobs in the city and were happy to support Ramesh's component of the rent till he found a job. This initiative encouraged Ramesh to keep an eye on the available rental accommodations around Sydney.

Initially, Ramesh tried the suburbs close to the city but after trying unsuccessfully for a few weeks, he decided to try looking for a place in the outer suburbs. He soon realised that even the outermost western suburbs were commanding astounding rents for meagre one-bedroom apartments. Each new day brought more disappointments and frustrations, and it came to a point where he just wanted to give up looking.

It was only by sheer chance that he came upon this property while surfing the internet. It was a house in Wallacia, a suburb in the far western regions of the city and situated close to the Nepean river. The redeeming feature was that it was a free-standing two-bedroom house and the rent was a fraction of any one-bedroom apartment in other suburbs. Although the house entailed long travel times for Luke and Marcello, Ramesh's infectious excitement soon convinced them to go and inspect the property.

Ramesh immediately booked an appointment with the real estate agency on the very next Saturday. The drive was long, but the excitement of actually getting a house on rent enlivened the spirits of the three young men. At the real estate agency, they were greeted by an over-indulgent representative who wasted no time in laying a brochure on the table that displayed a few photographs of the house together with a description of the attractive features of the house. After a short discussion, he offered to drive them to the house itself.

The house was much smaller than was portrayed in the photographs shown to them at the agency. It was a petite weatherboard structure built over a 400-square-metre plot. It had two small bedrooms, a living room and a minuscule kitchen. It even had a car port and a quaint porch in the front. It was on a quiet street and was flanked by two solid brick houses. The house had an old structure but looked neat despite its age. The trio fell in love with the old world charm of the house and before the hour had passed, they were back at the real estate agency office and putting pen to paper.

Within a week, all formalities having been completed, the three friends started packing. Since the house was available for immediate possession, they decided to move into their new abode within a week. A small and cheap removalist was hired and the contents of the apartment were moved to the new house without any incident except a slight dent to the refrigerator.

It was a sunny Saturday in Wallcia, as Marcello's rickety old jalopy came to a screeching halt before the house. From then on, the entire weekend was consumed with the activities usually associated with setting up a new house. The excitement drove Marcello and Luke to buy new furniture that they could ill afford. As dusk settled on Sunday, the three friends were completely exhausted but in a very happy frame of mind. Since they had a reason to rejoice, Luke soon drove to the local bottle shop and brought back a carton of beer.

As they laid out the beer bottles on a little table on the porch, they were pleasantly surprised by a friendly 'Hi' from the garden next door.

A big burly man was leaning over the fence and waving out to them. 'Hi,' the friendly giant growled. 'My name's Brian. Welcome to your new house.'

Luke waved back and said, 'Come and join us for a beer, mate.'

There was no need for a second invitation. The friendly giant strolled over to the porch and pulled up a chair for himself. After the initial formalities, the group got stuck into some well-earned drinks amidst a lot of bonhomie. The conversation drifted around the usual topics about the neighbourhood, work and other matters of life. In the end, the discussion came around to the house.

'Gee! It's good to see someone living in this house,' said Brian, in a slow rumbling voice.

Luke glanced at the others and asked, 'Has it been vacant for long?'

Brian wiped his mouth with the back of his hand. 'Yes,' he said. 'It's been vacant for nearly four years. The last tenant was a young family. They seemed to leave in a hurry.'

'What do you mean?' asked Marcello.

'Well,' Brian growled, reaching out for his second bottle of beer, 'they just left suddenly. They looked fine the day before when I spoke to them, and the very next day, I saw them packing their bags into the car and driving away. Never saw them again. I remember seeing a couple of removal vans come in a week later to move the furniture. Very strange.'

'Yes,' mused Luke, 'very strange indeed.'

'Did anyone live here before them?' Ramesh asked. There was a touch of concern in his voice.

'Wouldn't know that,' Brian replied. 'I moved in three months after the young family had taken up this house. You might as well ask Michael Hadley across the road. He's been here for nigh thirty years now. In fact, he owns this house.'

The revelation came as a surprise to the trio of friends.

'It's really curious that the agent made no mention of this,' Marcello said.

'Maybe Michael didn't want his name divulged,' Brian said. 'Some owners don't want their details revealed.'

The conversation then drifted to footy and cricket, which were obviously closer to Brian's heart and much more interesting than the history of the house.

It was nearly a week later when Ramesh first caught a glimpse of Michael Hadley across the road from the house. Although he seemed to be in his seventies, he looked much older. His wizened face had a pale sick look and he seemed to walk with a distinct limp. Ramesh quickly walked out to say a friendly hello to the old man. To his surprise, the old man quickly shuffled back into the house when he saw him approaching.

In the ensuing weeks, Ramesh was convinced that Michael Hadley was trying to avoid him. This came as a surprise to Marcello and Luke when Ramesh spoke about his encounters with the elusive landlord.

It was also around this time that Ramesh noticed that he felt quite cold inside the house, even during warm days. He spoke about this to his housemates but the comments were met with cynical remarks and wry smiles.

'Can't afford an air conditioner yet, mate,' Marcello said. 'Maybe we'll install one after you find a good job.'

The jibe did not go down well with Ramesh and he decided not to bring up the topic again.

Soon, the trio settled down in the house and life chugged along at a furious pace. Matthew and Marcello started having longer days due to the travel time to and fro from work. Ramesh started looking in earnest for a job at local businesses and soon found part-time work at a Woolworths outlet, not far from home.

Time, as they say, flies and four weeks went by in a flash.

It was the usual Friday evening session at the house and the trio prepared themselves for the consumption of beer and heaps of junk food. On this particular Friday, it was a KFC treat from Marcello, since he had had been promoted at work. The evening started early on the porch and after three hours of beer, chicken and fries, the friends decided to call it a day. As Marcello and Luke gulped down the last dregs from their bottles, Ramesh staggered towards the bathroom, slightly drunk.

Marcello and Luke retired into the living room to watch a popular

TV sitcom. The pair soon got engrossed in the tear-jerking episode and did not notice that Ramesh had not returned from the bathroom. It was only during the commercial break that Luke suddenly realised that Ramesh was not around.

'Hey, what's Ramesh up to?' Luke exclaimed. 'Did you see him go the bedroom?'

Marcello shook his head.

Luke grunted and looked at his watch. 'He's been there for more than thirty minutes.'

'Must have passed out,' Marcello laughed. 'Ramesh isn't used to six bottles of beer in one go, I reckon. Go and have a peek, mate.'

Luke sighed and got up from the sofa. He walked to the bathroom and knocked loudly on the door. But there was no response of any kind from within.

'Ramesh! What's up, buddy?' Luke shouted. 'Are you OK?'

There was no noise from within except the soft noise of shuffling feet and a few groans.

Marcello hastily joined Luke. 'Ramesh,' he shouted. 'Please open the door.'

They looked at each other and exchanged cynical looks. Their knocking soon turned to big thumps. Luke started pushing hard on the old timber door and Marcello joined him after a few shouts. The pushing, shoving and shouting went on for nearly ten minutes before Marcello lost his patience.

'I'm going to break down the fucking door,' he screamed, banging his shoulder against the flimsy woodwork.

Within minutes, the door burst open at the hinges and the sight that met their eyes was beyond their wildest expectations.

Ramesh stood next to the toilet bowl, his trousers still around his ankles. There was stark terror in his eyes and his body was shaking uncontrollably. He simply stared at the toilet bowl and, at the sight of his friends, started mumbling incoherent profanities.

Marcello shook Ramesh by his limp shoulders and dragged him

out. As Ramesh collapsed on the carpet, Luke knelt down beside him and put his ear close to his mouth trying to decipher the mumblings.

Ramesh remained stretched on the carpet, his shaking hand pointing at the toilet bowl. 'The hand,' he said in a voice that was hardly audible. 'The hand!'

'What is he talking about?' yelled Marcello. 'Has he gone bloody crazy or what?'

Luke moved his face closer to Ramesh's, his voice nearly a scream. 'What hand?'

'There was a hand in there.' Ramesh was nearly shrieking now. 'The hand...it pushed me up from the toilet. My God! The hand pushed me.'

Marcello walked up to the toilet bowl and peered in. 'Is he fucking crazy?' he asked, glancing into the toilet bowl. 'What fucking hand is he talking about?' He let out a nervous laugh.

Ramesh, in the meanwhile, was making furious gestures with his hand towards the toilet bowl, asking Marcello to sit on the bowl. Marcello looked at him with a disbelieving smile on his face as he sat down with a thud on the bowl and smiled apprehensively at the other two.

'You look funny, mate,' Luke said.

Ramesh just looked on, his mouth agape as a dribble of saliva rolled down his chin.

Marcello sat there for a few minutes. Then the cynical smile vanished from his face as he jumped up, shrieking profanities, his eyes fluttering in disbelief. The shake in his voice and body was unmistakable. 'He's bloody right, Luke.' Marcello's voice was hoarse with nervousness. 'A blasted hand just gave me a shove on the bum.'

Luke stared at him for a few seconds and then darted into the bathroom. He looked down into the dark toilet bowl and suddenly stark fear gripped at his heart. He could hardly speak. 'Let's get out of this place,' he managed to croak.

'Where the hell can we go at this hour?' screamed Marcello.

'I want to get out of this cursed place,' Ramesh wailed as he found his voice.

'Shut up everyone,' Luke shouted. 'We can't go anywhere at this time of night. We'll spend the night here and get out first thing in the morning.'

The three friends walked out on unsteady feet into the living room and sat huddled in the dimly lit room clutching at each other.

Their neighbour's words seemed to weave through their numbed minds like a movie in slow motion. *The last tenants were a young family who seemed to leave in a hurry. They looked fine the day before when I spoke to them and the very next day, I saw them packing their bags into the car and driving away.*

Even Ramesh, in his state of shock, realised why the landlord living across the road had turned his back upon them. Michael Hadley knew. No wonder the house was cheap to rent... It all started adding up.

They had no idea how the hours passed as they went in out of slumber. There was no word spoken and the silence of the night was only broken by the hard breathing of three terrified souls. At the very break of dawn, the three jumped into the car with their essential valuables and some belongings and drove off at what can be best described as breakneck speed.

A week later, Brian from the house next door saw a group of packers arrive to take away the rest of the belongings from the house. After that, he never heard from the three friends or from the agent and the house remained vacant thereafter.

Six years later, after Michael Hadley passed away, the house was sold as a deceased estate and ultimately purchased by a builder for a song. The house was torn down and excavations started immediately making space for a brand-new multi-storey structure to be built on top.

It was a late afternoon, during the excavations, when the builder received a call from one of the workers at the site. Apparently, while digging, they had just dug come upon a skeleton in an upright position from underneath the bathroom. The neck was broken at several places, indicating foul play. Strangely enough, one of the skeleton's hands was found to be stretched upwards, the palm facing the spot where the toilet bowl had been located.

The Healthy Man

Girdhar Rao arrived on the shores of Australia in the early part of 2005 and decided to call Perth his home. In India, after his decision to migrate to Australia, he was advised by friends to settle in Sydney since the city offered exciting opportunities for new settlers. However, Girdhar was an engineer by profession and he chose Perth because the city was in the midst of a mining boom. He was not far from the truth and he quickly settled into a new job with a mining company situated just outside the city. He spent his time between his job and his only other passion in life – health and fitness. Girdhar was a fitness fanatic and was very proud of the fact that he had never been to a doctor in the last six years. He spent his spare time in a myriad of fitness activities. He never missed his early morning run and also enrolled in a local gym. His lifestyle was meticulously ordered around his work and his fitness. He also nurtured a hope in his heart that one day he would have a partner who was as healthy and fitness-conscious as he was.

After three years, Girdhar decided to get married. He had accumulated a tidy saving in his bank account and had already started looking around for a small apartment for himself. It took him nearly two months to find the right home: a two-bedroom apartment near a railway station and, more importantly, close to a gym. After settling into his new home, Girdhar spoke to his parents, Hemchandra and Lalitha, in India about his wish to get married.

Since he was from a traditional south Indian Brahmin family, he had already decided to abide by the strict social rules and regulations that were applied to all marital alliances and was quite happy when Hemchandra informed him that they would look for a suitable bride for him. Girdhar had only one condition about his marriage, though.

He wanted his parents to make sure that the girl was a healthy lady and if possible, interested in fitness and general well-being. Knowing their son's penchant for a healthy lifestyle, Hemchandra and Lalitha gladly accepted their son's stipulation. After that, they started their search for a prospective bride and within three weeks they landed up four potential young ladies for their son. After the dowry negotiations were settled with each of them, Hemchandra called his son and asked him to book his flight to their hometown, Pandhipuram.

Pandhipuram was a very small town. In fact, Girdhar always felt that it was more of a large village than a small town and the village was agog with excitement when the news spread that Girdhar would be coming back to get married. It was big news for most of the townsfolk because he was the only person from the village to have migrated overseas. Most of them had heard stories about him from his parents and within the small community he had acquired a status that was nothing less than that of a celebrity. Hence, his parents were hardly surprised when a huge crowd gathered at the local railway station on the day that Girdhar landed at Pandhipuram. It was a warm April evening when Girdhar stepped off the train and into the waiting arms of his parents, who stood proudly among a sea of visitors, many of whom put garlands around Girdhar's neck, as was the tradition and custom in India.

After a few days of rest, Hemchandra organised appointments for the selected ladies and their families to visit his son. Separate evenings were set aside for each of the visiting families and the agenda remained exactly the same. The girl would arrive with her parents (and, at times, some accompanying elders from the family) and would then sit coyly on one side while her parents discussed details with Girdhar and his parents. After that, a big spread of food would be laid out for everyone and then, after a few smiles and nudges, the girl would be granted some private time to talk to Girdhar in another room. While some of the prospective brides did manage to ask a few questions about Girdhar's work and life in Australia, most of them were too shy to talk. In any case, most of the questions were from the prospective groom himself.

Girdhar remained cautious with all the ladies and generally focused on their ability to cook and their educational qualifications. He always kept his favourite question till the end and this was about their health and fitness. From each of his discussions and meetings, Girdhar took meticulous notes in a little brown diary. Later, after the guests had left, he would then sit down and browse through his notes till late at night.

The interviews went on for nearly a week, at the end of which Girdhar remained quite confused. It took him nearly an entire day to select two girls and he then requested his parents to pick one of them. Hemchandra and Lalitha had no hesitation in choosing a girl by the name of Pushpa and their choice was graciously accepted by Girdhar.

After this seemingly innocuous selection process, the wedding preparations started in earnest since Girdhar had only fifteen days left before his departure to Australia. The fact that his parents had already decided the date and venue for the wedding and had preselected a guest list (which incorporated nearly the entire village) made things easier. The priest was briefed, the caterers were advised and the invitations were sent out quickly.

The wedding day came and passed with only the expected hitches and chaos, and within ten days, Girdhar found himself to be a married man. His departure to Australia was marked by another large gathering at the railway station; a sober one this time with plentiful of tears, hugs and blessings.

Girdhar was soon on the flight to Perth.

The first duty for Girdhar, after he landed in Australia, was to apply for permanent residency for his spouse and since he had come well prepared with the prerequisite documents, the application was lodged without any glitches. Within three months, Pushpa landed in Perth and went about settling into the new phase of their lives. Within two weeks of her arrival, Girdhar got her to start applying for jobs and also showed her around Perth, getting her acclimatised to the Australian lifestyle.

Initially, it was a little hard for Pushpa to get used to the systems and the way of life in her new homeland, but within a year she settled in very well; her life balanced finely between household chores and a part-time job at the local supermarket. Girdhar made sure that she enrolled at the local gym and worked on a strict exercise schedule. He also took her for his long brisk walks around the suburbs. This was also the time when she found that she was pregnant.

It would have been a very joyous time for the couple except that it came to light that Pushpa had acute diabetes. The condition was uncovered when Girdhar took her to the local GP for a regular check-up. This startling discovery came as a huge blow to Girdhar and soon his worries turned to anger when he was informed by the doctor that this was a pre-existing condition that Pushpa might have developed years ago. On querying Pushpa further on the issue, Girdhar discovered that she had been aware of her condition but had kept it under covers, at the behest of her parents and her in-laws.

Girdhar felt betrayed and disappointed. He realised that his wife was not the healthy woman that he always wanted to have as a partner and he laid the blame squarely on his parents. Things turned quite sour in the household as he constantly worried about Pushpa's condition. Soon his moods turned foul. A wife with diabetes. This was the ultimate disappointment for him; he who had always put health ahead of everything else in life. His attitude changed at home, with frequent angry outbursts that ended in quarrels with Pushpa. As days passed by, his verbal abuses brought Pushpa to the edge of a mental breakdown. It was an untenable and unimaginable situation for the couple when his angry outbursts increased to a point where he could no longer control himself.

Amidst protests from Pushpa, he finally called his parents and confronted them over the phone. Over a heated exchange, his suspicions were confirmed. His parents did have prior knowledge about Pushpa's condition but had kept it from him since the dowry offered by Pushpa's parents was an extremely attractive one. The state of affairs was unacceptable for Girdhar. Living with a partner who did not conform to his levels of health was an unendurable thought. Without further ado and ignoring pleas from his friends and relatives in India, he soon put Pushpa on a one-way flight to India. He then contacted an old school friend in India who was a well-known divorce lawyer, and applied for divorce.

Girdhar then continued with his life that revolved around work and fitness. He refused to keep in touch with Pushpa and refused to enquire about the state of her pregnancy. It took him over a year to get the divorce papers successfully passed through the courts in India, at the end of which he felt that he was a free man and that he could do as he chose. He was, of course, constantly bombarded with phone calls from his parents urging him to remarry. He refused to do so and rebuffed the idea of falling into another trap in India. Instead, he decided to marry the girl of his choice, if he ever found one.

And he did. In fact, at the very gym that he frequented every day.

Neeta was an Australian-born Indian girl and her friendship with Girdhar blossomed at the gym based on common interests. Like him, she also had two simple pursuits in life – work and fitness. However, there was more to it. Like Girdhar, she was also an engineer and was equally fascinated and sometimes even fixated about things pertaining to health and well-being. And this suited Girdhar very well indeed. Their friendship turned to courtship within a few months, once Girdhar had made sure (very tactfully of course) that Neeta had no major medical conditions that could cause any concern in the future. Girdhar wasted no time in proposing to Neeta and then informed his parents about this rather momentous occasion in his life. At last, he felt that he was in control of his life and his aspirations about living healthy seemed to be a reality now. Within six months, the couple got married at a very quiet ceremony attended by a handful of local friends.

Life started very well for the couple. During the day, they would be very busy at work and in the evening they would meet up at the local gym for a solid two-hour workout. The food at home was, as expected, healthy and a supplement to their lifestyle. The weekends would be either spent in the company of some good friends or devoted to long runs around Perth. They refrained from alcohol, shunned fast foods of all varieties, subscribed to health magazines and encouraged their friends to adopt a healthy lifestyle. From their savings, they soon set up a small gym at home and spared no expense for the costly equipment which they often showed off to the envy of their other health-conscious friends. He also never tired of boasting to his friends that he had never seen a doctor since the day he put his foot on Australian soil.

Yes, life was certainly full of happiness for the couple and it would have continued to be a joyous one except for an unexpected fatality. Six months after their wedding, at the healthy age of thirty-five, Girdhar suddenly passed away, dropping dead as a result of a massive heart attack at the gym.

Girdhar's body had to be handed over to the coroner given the nature of his accidental death at a public place. After a few days of investigation, Neeta received a letter from the coroner's office. The letter stated that Girdhar had died of a chronic pre-existing heart condition that could have gone back to his teenage years and that he had a very healthy body but an extremely unhealthy heart.

The Prediction

Lax Iyengar had a very happy life. He was what is often referred to as a 'nine-to-five common man'. He worked with the New South Wales government as a senior clerk in the department of finance and was extremely happy with his work. His wife, Parimala, stayed at home and looked after the needs of Lax and the two kids. He was devoid of any ambition and the only expectation he had from life was to be able to retire peacefully in a nice suburb in Sydney.

Lax had arrived in Australia with his family, in the early 90s, his passport declaring him as Laxman Thiruvenkatraghava Iyengar. He was quick to realise that the first thing that he needed to do was change his name to a more pronounceable one. Soon he changed his name to Lax Iyengar and then, with an eye on the future, he decided to call his two sons Pat and Mike. Since then, life had been good to him in Australia, although he could not afford some of the expensive luxuries of life. Sometimes, on rare occasions, Lax secretly pined for some of those indulgences.

It was in the year 2000 that Lax suddenly, and unexpectedly, came into a large inheritance. His only maternal aunt in India had passed away, leaving behind an enormous inheritance that, even after converting to Australian currency, amounted to a very substantial sum. Life, for Lax, changed in a flash. After lengthy discussions with his wife, he decided to invest the money in the stock market for their future. However, Lax was a very religious and superstitious man and before making further decisions, he was adamant about consulting an astrologer.

He was referred by a friend to a Fijian-Indian astrologer by the name of Ram Prasad, who was visiting his son in Australia. Ram Prasad had a glowing track record and his visit to Australia had been widely publicised in the Indian newspapers. However, Lax was warned that the services from this venerable gentleman were quite expensive. Of course, money was no longer a problem for Lax and, without wasting time, he got himself an appointment with the esteemed astrologer.

A few days before the meeting, Lax received a phone call from Ram Prasad's son and was asked to send in the details of his birth to the astrologer. This included elements like the date of birth and place of birth that were often included in astrological equations. Lax diligently complied with the request and went to see Ram Prasad on the appointed day.

It was 1 July 2000 and Lax's meeting with the astrologer was to be major a turning point in his life.

Upon his arrival, Lax was greeted warmly by Ram Prasad and was quickly led into the spacious living room. Lax observed happily that the walls of the room were lined with framed photographs of several Indian gods and deities. After a few cordial exchanges, Ram Prasad got down to business quickly. He produced a sheaf of handwritten notes and browsed through them as Lax waited with mounting impatience.

After a few agonising moments, Ram Prasad looked up with a serious expression on his face. 'Can I please look at the palm of your right hand?' he asked.

Lax quickly extended his palm and waited with bated breath while Ram Prasad peered into his palm.

After a few minutes, Ram Prasad let go of Lax's palm and closed his eyes with a grave sigh. 'I have bad news for you, my friend,' he said at last. 'Very bad news.'

Lax's throat felt dry as he waited Ram Prasad to make his announcement.

'You do not have much long to live, I am afraid.' Ram Prasad's voice had fallen to a quiet whisper.

Lax found his voice with great difficulty. 'What do you mean?'

'You have just six more months left,' Ram Prasad said. 'I am sorry.'

'Are you sure?' asked Lax. He could hardly breathe. 'You might have made a mistake. Please check your calculations again. Please.'

Ram Prasad looked at him disdainfully. He shook his head. 'I do not make mistakes, Mr Iyengar,' he said. 'I have made this prediction after many hours of calculations. The lines on your palm have also confirmed my prophecy. I would request you please prepare for your future. All calculations show that the date might be 31 December this year.'

Lax tried to say something but it seemed that he had lost his voice.

'It is rather sad,' Ram Prasad continued. 'But then, such is life. I am sorry about this. Would you like to know about the other predictions for your family that I have derived?'

Lax shook his head as he felt his world explode around him. He realised that the meeting had come to an end as Ram Prasad stood up and shook his hand.

Ram Prasad looked at him kindly. 'You can make your payment to my son Mick on your way out. He is in the outer room.'

The next few days were like an unending nightmare for Lax and Parimala. While Lax took leave from work, he hardly spoke to Parimala, who wept incessantly. The children were, of course, kept in the dark since Lax did not want to burden their young lives with the disastrous news. After three days, Lax made a firm decision. He was a blind believer in the predictions of the stars and he wanted to make the most of his short life in the next six months.

On the fourth day after his meeting with Ram Prasad, he quit his job and booked four tickets around the world. Within the next three weeks, he also purchased a very large and modern house, in a good suburb, that was available for immediate sale and possession. Then he went about diligently looking for a good car and bought himself a Mercedes. After that, he spent a very large sum buying expensive amenities for his new house. He also asked Parimala and his children to stock their wardrobes with new garments.

Within the next two months, Lax set sail around the world with his family. It was a wonderful time for them and lasted nearly two months. The aura of happiness and content nearly made Lax forget about his impending death. However, after his return, the gloom settled in again and the only panacea for Lax was to spend more money and enjoy the final vestiges of his life. There was hardly a day when the family did not eat out at expensive restaurants. Lax forced himself to develop a liking for fine wines and the races. He bought expensive gifts for the family, frequented good pubs and regularly entertained his friends. Life and its unforeseen calamities had indeed changed him.

The month of December approached at a quicker pace than Lax had imagined. During the last week of the month, he woke up every morning with the uncomfortable thought of not waking up the next day. Both Lax and Parimala seemed to have lost the urge to sleep. They stayed up nights and could hardly be at peace during the day. The dreadful days passed by at an agonisingly slow pace, as they waited for the impending doom.

To their surprise, 31 December came and went passed without any incident.

After that, the days changed to weeks and then into months. Lax did not die. In fact, he felt better than ever. But the spending did not stop. It was an incurable habit by then. After six months, he accepted the fact that death was definitely not coming up to knock at his door.

Of course, the money had dried up by then and, in fact, there was a large debt riding on Lax's shoulders. The only relief was that he had not informed the children about the prediction and in the process had spared them a lot of heartache. As the financial burdens increased, Lax sold his house and his car and then moved with the family into a small apartment in the far west of the city. He applied for countless jobs but in vain. Ultimately, Parimala took up a clerical job with a local car dealer in order to support the family.

The years passed by slowly. The children grew up into responsible adults and moved away to Melbourne for work. At home, Lax's life became a routine as he trained himself to cook and clean up the house while Parimala was away at work. Life chugged along without any major incident and the years flew by.

It was nearly twelve years later, by sheer coincidence, that the memories of Lax's encounter with the astrologer were revived. It happened during dinner at a friend's house. It was a large gathering and the host had taken upon himself to introduce Lax to some of the guests. Lax's curiosity was aroused when he came upon a Fijian-Indian gentleman by the name of Mick who looked vaguely familiar. The level of curiosity was pushed up a notch when the gentleman was introduced as Mick Prasad. Since the name Prasad was indelibly etched in Lax's memory, he gathered some courage and approached Mick Prasad after dinner, for a casual conversation.

After an exchange of some general pleasantries, Lax carefully broached the topic. 'I was wondering,' he said, 'if you know an astrologer by the name of Ram Prasad from Fiji. I met him many years ago.'

Mick Prasad looked at Lax and raised his eyebrows in surprise. 'That's an odd coincidence,' he said with a smile. 'Of course I know him. I'm his son.'

Lax nearly passed out and barely managed to suppress an exclamation. He suddenly knew why Mick Prasad looked familiar. Mick looked much like his father and he was also the one who had collected the consultation fees on the day of the fateful meeting.

'That is indeed an amazing coincidence.' Lax managed to put on a dry smile. 'And where is he now?'

'Ah,' said Mick Prasad. 'Unfortunately he passed away many years ago.'

'Sorry to hear about that.' Lax tried to sound interested. 'And when was this?'

'He passed away in the year 2000, on 31 December.'

Lax gulped and then stared at Mick Prasad.

'Believe it or not,' Lax said. 'I met him in that same year. On 1 July 2000.'

'Really?' said Mick Prasad. 'Looks like Dad passed away exactly six months after he met you.'

The Street Hawker

It was by mere chance that I saw him.

This happened during my trip to Ahmedabad in India. Ahmedabad was my home town before I decided to move to Australia and call Sydney my new home. On that particular day, I was quite bored as it oft happens when you have spent the first hectic week meeting family members and catching up with old cronies. After my cup of morning tea and having nothing important on hand, I decided to take a stroll and stretch my legs. In India, it is extremely difficult to get any kind of exercise during the day given the fact that even taking a short stroll amidst the milling crowds hardly gives you the opportunity to pick up brisk speed. I, therefore, decided to take a leisurely stroll down a road that used to be the major commercial thoroughfare during my university days.

I hailed a rickshaw and got dropped off at the southern end of the road from where I wanted to start my walk. I took off at a fairly brisk pace and within twenty minutes I approached one of the oldest hospitals in the city known to most inhabitants as simply V.S. Hospital. The section of the road outside the hospital was traditionally the busier part of the road. Shops of every kind lined the road and the footpaths were in a state of perennial congestion due to the grinding crowds weaving their way through the street hawkers lining the street and selling a mind-boggling array of wares ranging from clothes, food to junk jewellery.

For me, the walk near the hospital was sheer nostalgia and brought back a myriad of memories from the years gone by. As I approached the hospital, I slowed down to a crawling pace as I tried to weave through the crowds and the street hawkers.

However, just outside the gates of the hospital, I stopped abruptly and looked back. In the throng, I had recognised a face. As often happens, you sometimes see a face from the past and tend to pass it at the first glance. Possibly it takes a few moments for the brain to decipher the cognition. As I looked back at the crowd, I could only see a maze of faces and nothing more. Curiosity, however, got the better of me and I decided to retrace my steps because I was sure that the familiar face was that of Mohanlal. As I walked back, I peered curiously at the faces of the hawkers much to their annoyance of course.

And then I came upon him. It was Mohanlal. He stood before a small *thelaa* – a hand-pulled cart popularly used by street hawkers in India – that was laden with cheap jewellery. As I walked up and stood before him, he looked up.

'Remember me? It's been twenty-five years,' I said.

He stared back at me, a blank look in his eyes. He looked emaciated and his face had a gaunt and hungry look. He was a far cry from the Mohanlal that I knew.

Was my imagination playing tricks or was that a glint of recognition in the hooded eyes?

He shook his head. 'No, can't seem to remember you, sahib.' His voice sounded harsh.

But I did remember him. Remembered him very well in fact.

During the days when I was struggling as a full-time musician, Mohanlal was one of the most sought-after impresarios in the state of Gujarat. In a world of an unending rat race, he was the leading rat. He held his cue over most major concerts in the market and ruled over the musicians with an iron fist. His name was often linked to the sleazy underbelly of the city and even speaking to him in those days was a daunting task. He regaled in the fact that he instilled a sense of fear among musicians.

The year was 1983 and Mohanlal had booked a few musicians for a series of six concerts around the state. I was one of the chosen ones.

Those were very hard times for me, given that I had to feed a family of four from the meagre income that music provided. Every concert mattered, as did every rupee. Mohanlal's six concerts were quite well spaced, with about a week separating each event held in different cities. Each concert was a roaring success with overflowing audiences. Mohanlal kept a friendly demeanour throughout the tour, possibly because of the money that he was raking in at each event. I was happily playing out the events with an eye on the promised contract amount that was to be paid to me, albeit upon the completion of the events.

Three days before the final concert, as I sat smoking one of my cheap cigarettes in a seedy hotel room, a fellow musician informed me that there was someone to see me downstairs in the hotel atrium. This was a complete surprise to me since I hardly knew a soul in that city. As I stepped into the worn-down lobby, I was approached by a well-dressed elderly man whom I had never seen before.

'Can I please speak to you in private?' he asked in a soft voice.

'You can talk here freely,' I replied looking around. 'There's no one around.'

He looked a little worried and insisted that we should go and talk in the street outside. I found this rather intriguing and once we stepped out, he wasted no time.

'Look, my name is Hiren Shah and I'm a producer of small concerts. I need to book you for one of my upcoming events.'

'What is the date of your concert?' I asked.

'I'm afraid that my concert date coincides with Mohanlal's final concert.'

I shook my head. 'I can't help you then. You need to look for another musician.'

He shook his head vehemently. 'I need your skills, my friend. I have tried others, but no one is available.'

'But how can I accept your offer? I have a contract with Mohanlal.'

His voice dropped a notch. 'Listen,' he pleaded. 'Make an excuse.'

I shook my head.

His voice almost dropped to a hushed whisper. 'I will pay you three times the money that Mohanlal pays you. This is a critical event for me and I need you. I will pay the entire amount in advance if you want. It will be quite easy because my event is in Porbandar, which is a long way from Ahmedabad. Mohanlal would not have an inkling.'

An extra rupee in those days meant a few more pieces of bread on the table for my family. It was not the extra money but the vision of those extra pieces of bread that drove me to accept Hiren Shah's concert.

Fortunately, Mohanlal's final concert was in my hometown. Three days before the event, I convinced one of my close friends to call in on my behalf and apologise to Mohanlal for my unavailability. I advised my friend to tread carefully and tell Mohanlal that I was very unwell. My good friend did what was required of him and I left town to travel to Porbandar to participate in Hiren Shah's concert.

In those days, the tradition was to get your outstanding payments from Mohanlal a few days after the completion of entire series of the concerts. After returning from Porbandar, I decide to wait for over a week before collecting my outstanding dues from Mohanlal. I vividly remember the damp monsoon day when I decided to go collect my outstanding money from him. My heart was quite heavy, weighed down with traces of trepidation. I landed up at the seedy café in the inner-city precinct of Ahmedabad, which was his usual haunt. Usually, one would be taken aside by his henchmen and the cash would be thrust into an eager palm. However, this time, I was taken aback when I was told that Mohanlal wanted to see me personally.

I waited for him with great anxiety and fear, hoping that I would not be chastised for missing his last concert. Did he know about my participation at Hiren Shah's event? Would I be dropped from future events?

However, what ensued was way beyond my expectation.

After what seemed to a long-drawn hour, I was beckoned to see Mohanlal. He was at his usual place at the head of the customary table.

As I pulled up a chair next to him, he turned around and faced me, his face inches away from mine.

'You fucking bastard,' he snarled. 'You thought you could cheat on me, behind my back.'

I shuddered. Obviously he knew that I had performed at another concert.

'I am very sorry,' I stammered. 'I needed the money.'

'And now,' he smirked, 'you will get nothing at all. Nothing. Not a rupee, you cheating bastard,'

His words were the beginning of a terrible fifteen minutes of physical abuse and verbal insults. At the end of the ordeal, I was physically removed from the café, beaten black and blue by his henchmen and then thrown out on to the grubby street. I remembered how I had pleaded and cajoled with them for the meagre sum of two hundred and fifty rupees. I just wanted the money for the concerts in which I had participated. Something that was legally due to me. Just two hundred and fifty rupees.

I recalled walking back home in tears. The tears flowed not for the insults and physical abuse but for the pain of impoverishment and sleepless nights that were sure to follow.

That incident with Mohanlal was to remain vividly etched in my memory for many years to come. Soon after that, I stopped working for Mohanlal and, in a few years, he seemed to slowly fade out of the scene amidst stories of drugs, financial ruin, massive debts and street brawls. Since that day at the café in 1983, I had never set eyes on Mohanlal till that fateful moment when I chanced upon him during my walk.

Mohanlal was still staring at me. I gave him my business card. He read out my name loudly and looked closely at me. This time, the faraway sparkle in the tired eyes did not escape me. I knew then that my imagination was definitely not playing tricks on me.

Mohanlal had recognised me. He shook his head and his eyes shifted away. 'Can't understand English, sahib,' he said in a slow whisper. 'But can I offer you some bangles? Maybe a few earrings, sahib?'

I looked at him and the vision of that fateful day at the café emerged briefly in front of my eyes. I pointed at the junk on his handcart. 'How much would that cost?' I asked him.

He looked back at me blankly.

'What's the cost of your entire stock?' I asked him, raising my voice a little.

The blank look was first replaced by a look of incredulity and was immediately overshadowed by a cunning one. 'That would be around two thousand rupees, sahib,' he said staring at me.

I dipped my hand in trouser pocket, my eyes never leaving his face. He had stopped looking at my face by then and his furtive eyes followed every move of my hands. I took out a bundle of notes, counted two thousand rupees and held out the pack towards him.

He looked straight into my eyes now. Gone were the blank look and the cunning stare. Instead, within the depth of the dark eyes, there lurked a gaze of nothingness and desolation that played hide and seek with sheer greed and sadness. In a sudden flurry of activity, he started dropping his ware into a big plastic bag.

I tapped him on the shoulders and he looked up with a jerk.

'I just want some bangles worth two hundred and fifty rupees,' I said.

'Two hundred and fifty rupees, sahib?' he asked, unable to fathom what I had said. He seemed to have frozen at one spot, unable to do anything.

'You just owe me two hundred and fifty rupees. Nothing more and nothing less,' I said, looking into his rheumy eyes.

Then I leaned forward and picked up ten of the twenty-five-rupee bangles from the cart and, after thrusting the bundle of notes in his claw-like palm, I turned and walked away.

'Sahib!' he cried after me. 'Sahib, please wait! *Mujhe sab kuchh yaad aa gayaa!* I remember everything now!'

I refused to look back. I did not want to look back. I simply kept on walking till I lost myself within the mulling crowd.

Mistletoe Creek

I looked up from my habitual seat on the little green bench near the water tap, as the train screeched to a grinding, aching halt at the Mistletoe Creek station. It was ten p.m. and the little platform was, as usual, deserted except for Jim, the old stationmaster. In the past forty years, Jim had truly become a part of the furniture.

Mistletoe Creek is a small town, situated in the heart of the Northern Territory. It has no more than five hundred inhabitants. In the early 40s, the town used to be a busy mining centre, pulsating with life and gold diggers. The gold rush had died down by the 50s but many obstinate families had hung on, living off the land and cattle. The town had ploughed on for the next decade amidst rising unemployment and financial woes.

Then, in 1971, came that train crash near the station, leaving hundreds dead in a raging inferno. The tragedy made international headlines and, although the cause of the accident never came to light, the consequences were dire for the little town. Nearly every inhabitant lost a dear one. And soon, the town had another stigma attached to it: that of being haunted. Reports about dead inhabitants being sighted were not uncommon and the innuendoes spread like wildfire. Within a span of a few months, the flow of visitors dried up except for the very curious or the very courageous. Burdened under the weight of the rumours, most of the inhabitants left for good, leaving behind the ones who were either fearless or had no other place to go. Jim, the stationmaster, was one of them and so was I.

As the handful of passengers started getting off the train, Jim walked past my little green bench and completely ignored me. He always did that and I found his attitude to be extremely irritating. He knew that I liked hanging around the station platform every night. Yet he never spoke to me. I suspect that he was wary of all foreigners, including Indians.

Yes, I am an Indian. One of the very early settlers in Australia. I migrated to Australia in 1968 and, having found no work in the bigger cities, I decided to move to a mining town in the Northern Territory. After loitering around in many small towns, I finally landed at Mistletoe Creek. As luck would have it, there were a few small mining companies who were looking for staff during that period and I soon landed up a job at a warehouse. My family then joined me from Adelaide, where I had left them before going on my job-hunting mission.

Our arrival in Mistletoe Creek was a bit of a cultural shock for the inhabitants since the folk around town had not seen many 'brown skins' before our arrival. But they turned out to be a friendly lot and once the social hurdles were crossed, the townsfolk helped us settle in quickly. My wife, Gopi, found a job at a local grocer's and the kids enrolled at the local primary school. The only school in town, by the way.

I peered at the passengers who had just alighted from the train and was pleasantly surprised (and quite happy, I might add) to see among the passengers a well-built young man in his late twenties. It was rare to find one of the new generation coming into town and it always made me happy to see a young face. He was clad in jeans, sported a flashy maroon T-shirt and carried a couple of compact suitcases. He walked up to Jim and spoke to him, gesticulating towards the gate of the station. Jim replied briefly, shaking his head, and ushered him towards the bench next to the one where I sat. As the train whistled and prepared to depart, the young man walked towards me. As he came closer, I observed that he was looking curiously at my outdated clothes and faded leather shoes. It was obvious that the fashion of the 70s failed to create an impression upon the young man.

'Good evening,' he said.

'Hello.' I greeted him with a smile. 'Looking for someone?'

'Hell, yes,' he replied, looking around. 'My uncle was supposed to have been here to receive me.'

'He will be here soon, I am sure,' I said looking over my shoulder towards station's gate. I was glad that his uncle was running late because I rarely had the opportunity to talk to people.

'Name's Brian Selby,' he said with a smile. 'Mind if I sit down?'

I flashed a friendly 'don't mind at all' smile. 'I am Anand Kumar. Where are you from?' I asked.

'Sydney,' Brian replied, rolling his eyes. 'A far cry from this place, I can assure you.' He let out a hearty laugh and lit a cigarette. 'Would you like one?' he asked, looking down at my nicotine-stained fingers.

'Thank you,' I said, accepting his offer. Discarded cigarette butts were all that I could afford these days.

He smoked for a while in silence, glancing occasionally at the gate. Then he suddenly turned round and asked, 'Pretty quiet around here, isn't it? And haunted too, I heard.'

'Does that scare you?' I asked cautiously.

'No.'

'Good. Not all ghosts are bad, you know,' I remarked with a smile.

'Do you believe in the rumours?' He had a quizzical smile on his young face.

I stared at him for a few moments. 'I think there might be an element of truth in the rumours.'

Brian smiled wryly at me. 'Really?'

I just nodded and looked away. I did not want to discuss ghosts with the young man. The subject gave me no pleasure at all.

Brian, however, was quite intent on pursuing the subject. 'I don't believe in ghosts,' he said. 'Have you ever seen one?'

I did not want to tell him about the odd things I had seen in this town. Least of all, I did not want to scare away visitors that the town badly needed.

'My only ghosts are my memories,' I said.

'Hmm,' he mused. 'How long have you been here in this town? You would surely know my uncle. Fred Grundy.'

'Of course I know Fred. I've known him for the last forty years now,' I said, looking away towards the station gate.

'Forty years, did you say?' he asked. He was possibly surprised since I looked every inch an Indian.

'Yes,' I replied with a smile. 'Four decades. Seems like four years, to be honest.'

'You must one of the earliest Indians in this part of the world.'

'Yes, we were. We were the first Indians to tread into Mistletoe Creek.'

He must have seen the misty look in my eyes. He paused before the next inevitable question. 'Did you lose anyone in the 1971 train crash?' he asked.

My answer was a well-rehearsed one. 'Yes. I lost everyone in my family,' I replied, looking down.

'I am sorry,' he muttered under his breath.

An awkward silence ensued.

'Are you married?' I asked, just in order to divert attention away from the topic.

'Oh, yes,' he said proudly. 'We have a son. He's two years old.'

The discussion then wandered off to matters relating to family, friends and life in general. We spoke at length about travels to distant lands, argued about politics and discussed food and sports. I asked him many questions about Sydney and Melbourne since I had seen those cities many decades ago. Brian turned out to be a great conversationalist and I enjoyed every moment of his company. In fact, with every passing minute, I yearned for more. I wanted the conversation to go on forever.

I knew that Fred Grundy would arrive any moment and I surely did not want Fred to see me talking to the young man. My reputation in town was rather tarnished. I also felt the stationmaster's eyes boring into my back, from his little tumbledown office. It was time for me to leave. I pretended to look at my broken watch that had stopped thirty-five years ago. I stood up and extended my hand and the young man grasped it with youthful exuberance.

'It's getting late. Have to move on now,' I said with a smile. 'I'm sure Fred will be here very shortly. Otherwise, you can always speak to Jim the stationmaster. He'll help you out.'

'See you around town,' he replied. 'I'll be sticking around for a week.'

'Bye,' I said and turned away. I'd be sticking around forever.

'Hopefully, I'll see a ghost too,' Brian said with a laugh, as I walked away.

Limping badly on my shattered limbs, I started walking away quickly into the eternal darkness just as Fred Grundy walked into the station.

I felt dejected because I had walked away from an unfinished conversation with the young man. I wanted to say a lot more to him. I wished I could tell him that he wouldn't see me around the town and that he would always see me after dark, on the little green bench at the station. I also wanted to tell him that his uncle Fred and the stationmaster Jim knew me not because I was an old Indian inhabitant of the town. They knew me because I had perished with my family, in that fatal train crash in 1971...the only Indian family to have ever perished in a train accident in the 70s.

Brian wanted to see a ghost. I wished I could tell him that he had already seen one.

The Affordable Private Investigator

Kuldip Singh often boasted that he was quite unique among the entire Indian community in Melbourne. Dippy Singh (as he called himself professionally) was a private investigator and, in his opinion, the only PI in Australia with an Indian background.

Difficult circumstances had forced Dippy into this intriguing profession. He had migrated to Australia as a software programmer in the year 2000 and had found an excellent job within two weeks of his arrival. However, over the next few years the demand for his skills had gone into a decline. Unable to keep up with changing environments in technology, he soon found himself without a job. Most of the permanent positions were being outsourced to other countries and there were hardly any options left for him. He did manage to get a few good contracting positions with local companies but time and again he found himself in job queues. Dippy was never one to procrastinate and had always prided himself on his ability to think laterally, an ability that surfaced whenever he was forced into a corner. He decided to become a private investigator. He had never heard of or come across an Indian detective in Australia and therein he saw his opportunity.

Dippy enrolled in the compulsory certificate III course in investigative services and passed the exams with flying colours. Luckily, he found a job at one of the largest private investigative agencies in Melbourne, which was looking for people with ethnic backgrounds. Dippy worked very hard and put in countless long hours learning various aspects of the trade. His only ambition was to start his own business, which he did after a two-year stint at the agency. He leased a small office located in the heart of a well-known Indian suburb in Melbourne and proudly put up a sign that stated in large red letters,

Dippy Singh
The Affordable Private Investigator

The word 'affordable', as expected, worked miracles among local Indians, who were always on the lookout for a bargain, whether it be groceries or a private investigator. The word spread quickly within the community and before long, Dippy had an interesting Indian clientele who needed a wide range of services: investigations into fraud, background checks, monitoring teenager activities and inquiries into cheating partners (the most popular one). Within a couple of years, Dippy had established himself as one of the most well-known people in the Indian community and often rubbed shoulders with people from the influential and affluent quarters of the society. He postponed getting married for personal reasons that he refused to discuss with anyone and spent all his time working in his office and remaining dedicated to a profession that he found interesting and quite rewarding.

It was a bright summer morning and Dippy was making himself the first cup of coffee when he heard the bell ring at the door. Since he had never wanted to employ a secretary or a receptionist, he always kept the front door locked. This worked very well because his regular clients always saw him by appointment while walk-in clients would be forced to ring the large doorbell outside the glass doors.

'Damn,' Dippy Singh muttered under his breath. He was never keen on seeing anyone before his first coffee of the day.

Dippy opened the door with a flourish (one of the techniques that often impressed his customers) and then quickly took a stock of the Indian man standing outside. The man was bald, in his mid-forties, and his shirt buttons were struggling against a bulging midriff. He looked very worried. Dippy loved worried looks on clients since it always augured well for his business.

'Singh. Dippy Singh,' he said extending his hand. 'Please come in.'

Dippy made a mental note of the clammy and wet hand that he held during the brief handshake. As he stood aside to let the man pass through, he also made a quick note of the dirty shirt collar and loose trousers. He then led his prospective client into his personal chamber and pointed towards a comfortable chair across the table. The man sat down gingerly on the edge of the chair and looked at Dippy. There was a hunted look about the man.

He extended his limp hand towards Dippy as if he had forgotten that they had shaken hands a moment ago. 'Forgot to introduce myself,' he said apologetically. 'Tony Vaz.'

Dippy stared at the man. After a few seconds, he asked, 'How can I help you?'

Tony Vaz did not waste any time and came to the point with a singular statement. 'I think my wife is having an affair and I need to know who it is,' he said in a husky voice.

'Are you conjecturing about this or are you absolutely sure?' Dippy asked, pulling a writing pad towards him.

'I have no proof,' said Tony. 'But I know. My instincts cannot be wrong. I want you to please find out if this is true.'

'Firstly, I need some information from you. You need to tell me about your wife and a few details about your address and your contact details,' Dippy said, and started writing his notes even before Tony's response.

Tony had been married to Cheryl for over fifteen years. They lived in the quaint suburb of Aberfeldie and had a great life that had, of course, turned topsy-turvy once Tony had inklings about his wife's affair. His first suspicions were aroused when she started coming home late from work, several times a week; something that she had no need to do since she was only a receptionist at a large firm. She had explained the late nights as 'added responsibilities' at work. However, after a few discreet inquiries, he had managed to find out from her workplace that she never had to work late. Later, she had brushed aside his allegations with disdainful smiles and told him repeatedly that she worked in a large company and that he had been given inaccurate information. However, one night he had smelt a whiff of an unknown male perfume on her and the incident had forced him to go looking for a private investigator. He had looked up in the Yellow Pages and was thrilled to have found an Indian name among the list of investigators.

As Tony reclined back into the chair after his soliloquy, Dippy completed his notes and scanned through the details with a frown. 'Are you sure that she hasn't joined a gym or a class of some sort?' he asked at last.

Tony sat up with a scowl. 'No, she has not,' he growled. 'She's seeing someone, for heaven's sake.'

Dippy nodded wisely and said, 'Before we proceed, I need to tell you that my first consultation is free and I'll start sending you my invoices after I've made some progress.'

'And when would that be?' Tony asked.

'In the next couple of weeks.'

'Couple of weeks?' The urgency in Tony's voice had gone up a notch now. 'This is an urgent matter. I'm happy to pay extra money for your immediate services.'

Dippy looked at Tony closely and observed the beads of sweat on the forehead. 'That's fine, Tony,' he said, getting up. 'I'll consider this matter as urgent and get back to you in two to three days if that's OK with you.'

Tony Vaz let out a sigh and stood up shakily. There was a look of relief on his face. 'Thank you,' he said and walked out of the office.

Dippy sat down and held his head in his hands for a while. 'Interesting. Very interesting,' he muttered under his breath. 'Need to make a meticulous plan for this one.'

Tony Vaz called Dippy's office after two days, to ask about his progress.

'There hasn't been much progress yet,' Dippy told him. 'I'm just making some early inquiries at Cheryl's workplace.'

'You need to do more,' Tony's voice sounded desperate over the phone. 'She's done it again. She came back home at eleven last night. She has never been that late.'

'Just calm down, Tony,' Dippy said. 'I'll start trailing her movements within the next few days.'

After a week, Dippy called Tony on his mobile number. 'No progress yet, Tony,' Dippy told him. 'I've trailed her from her work every day to the station. All she does is to get into the train heading towards your suburb. Has she been coming home late?'

'No,' Tony replied in a very soft voice. 'In fact, she's been coming home quite early. Is it possible that she knows that she's being trailed?'

'Impossible,' Dippy replied. 'Listen. Just stay calm and let me keep a tab on her for another week.'

'But she hardly even talks to me these days. And that damned perfume. I smelt it on her again.' Tony sounded very agitated.

'You need to calm down.' Dippy tried to sound as convincing as he could. 'Wait for my call sometime next week.' Dippy ended the call before Tony could continue.

However, Tony called back again in three days. This time he called Dippy on his mobile number, late in the evening. 'I'm sorry that I had to call again.'

Dippy could hear a slur in Tony's voice.

'She came back very late last night.'

'Have you been drinking, Tony?' Dippy asked, even though he knew the answer.

'I'm sorry,' Tony wailed over the phones. There was a tremor in his voice. 'I just can't handle this anymore. Yes, I am drinking. Drinking a lot more than I should. Have you found anything?'

'Nothing at all,' Dippy said. 'She just catches the train back home every day. She did that yesterday too. I've been getting on to the train with her. She gets off at the Aberfeldie station each time.'

There were a few seconds of silence before Tony replied. 'It means that she's seeing someone after she gets off the train. Damn it! I want you to follow her after she gets off the train.'

'Please get a grip on yourself, Tony,' Dippy said in a firm voice. 'Can you please see me in two days, at my office? I need to give you my invoice and also discuss the plan for the future.'

Two days later, Dippy was shocked to see Tony's state as he entered the office. The man looked bedraggled and unshaven and there was an unmistakable stench of liquor on his breath. After Tony settled down gingerly in the usual overstuffed chair, Dippy looked at him closely and noticed the slight shake in his hands. 'Tell me frankly, Tony,' he said. 'Have you always had a drinking problem?'

'Yes, I have had problems before. But what has this got to do with the situation?'

'Look, I need to know a few things about you so that I can help you out. Have you ever been violent with her?'

'Fuck everything!' Tony screamed. 'I can't handle this any longer. I'll kill myself one of these days or kill someone.'

'That's an extreme statement.' Dippy was taken aback. 'I just wanted to know what could have triggered Cheryl's behaviour.'

'Do you think my drinking problems have triggered this? And yes, I've been accused of domestic violence once before, if that appeases your needs. But what's that got to do with this case?' Tony was nearly screaming.

Dippy stared at Tony. He could see the underlying foul temper being fuelled by alcohol.

'Look, I need answers or I'll kill myself.' Tony was rambling under his breath now.

Then he suddenly dug into his trouser pocket and produced a huge wad of hundred-dollar notes. 'Take it all,' he said. 'Just get me answers. Follow her day and night, if you have to. Do whatever's needed. Money's not a problem for me. I'll call you in three days.'

With those words, Tony just got up and left the office without waiting for a reply.

Dippy looked after his retreating figure with a faraway look in his eyes. 'What do I do next?' he said to himself. 'What's next?'

Tony called Dippy the very next morning and the latter immediately sensed the urgency in the slurred voice.

Tony was shouting into the phone. 'It's a different perfume now. A fucking different perfume.'

'Hang on,' Dippy said. 'Please calm down. What do you mean?'

'I smelt a different male perfume on her. This is not the one that I smelt before. Is she seeing different men?'

'That's a bit too far-fetched, Tony,' Dippy said. 'It might be that the man has changed his perfume, for heaven's sake. That is if she is really seeing someone.'

'What the hell do you mean? Of course, she's seeing someone. God, this is killing me. I feel suicidal. I want to kill myself.'

'No, you won't do anything like that.' Dippy's voice was very firm.

'If you don't get answers, I'll slit my throat.'

'You're being stupid, Tony. It will spoil all our efforts if she gets on her guard. I'm confident that we'll get a breakthrough very soon.' Dippy heard a sob at the other end. 'Just hang in there,' he said. 'Come and see me in a week. Give me some time to work things out for you.'

He heard a click as Tony disconnected the line. Then he sat back into the chair, his eyes closed. He let out a long sigh. He needed to work out a proper plan now. Too much procrastination might not be beneficial for anyone in this case. He wanted to give himself at least three to four days before making the next move.

Dippy's wish was far too optimistic. Two days later, when he arrived at work, he found Tony sitting on the polished tiled floor outside his office. As he walked up, Tony looked up him through rheumy eyes. It was almost a pleading look.

'She doesn't want to share my bedroom any more. This is it. The final proof.'

Tony looked shocking. He was shaking and had bloodshot eyes. Dippy could smell the liquor again; much stronger now. Dippy helped him to his feet and led him into the office.

'You need to get a grip on yourself, my friend,' Dippy said. 'You have to see someone about your mental state first. You need medical help.'

'I already have,' Tony said, sinking into a chair. His voice was hardly audible. 'I've seen a GP and I've been seeing a shrink. I'm falling apart, man. Please help me. Please.'

Dippy looked at the broken man. 'I have some news for you, Tony.'

Tony's eyes brightened up for a moment and he looked hopefully at Dippy.

'She was with a man last night,' declared Dippy. 'At the central station.'

'I knew it,' Tony shouted, jumping up on his feet. 'Do you know who the man was?'

'She was with a tall man; very dark and sporting a moustache.'

'That's all? Do you seriously think I can identify the man with that kind of a description?' Tony shrieked. 'I know scores of Indian men who fit that description. I need more information.' He took out a flask and gulped as streams of whiskey dribbled down. 'Get me his address. I will not tolerate this any more. I'll kill her.' Tony's voice was croaking with emotion.

'No, you won't kill anyone, Tony,' said Dippy. 'We're very close to the truth now. For heaven's sake, don't be reckless. We need that final proof before we nail her.'

Tony looked at him helplessly and a tear trickled down his face. For the first time, Dippy felt pity for Tony as he slowly ambled towards the door on unsteady feet. Dippy watched him leave the office, then went and shut the door. Suddenly he wanted to go home and rest for a while. He felt that he needed a break from the chaos. But there was much to be done. He left his office and headed towards the central station in search of Cheryl.

Next day, Dippy called Tony on his mobile at ten a.m. The phone rang for a long time before Tony answered. Dippy could hardly recognise the voice. It was the voice of a man at breaking point.

'She didn't come home last night,' Tony said. 'The bitch!'

'Have you informed the police?' asked Dippy cautiously.

'No, I haven't.'

'Good,' Dippy replied. 'Come down to my office immediately. I have a lot of information that might help you.'

'I don't have the time to come down. I want to know now,' Tony said.

'I don't know who the man is. But I can assure you that she was with the same man last evening. Like last time, she caught a train with him to Parktown.' Dippy could only hear heavy breathing at the other end. 'There's more,' he continued. 'This time, I noticed two interesting things about the man. He had a large mole on his right cheek and a distinctive limp.'

Dippy heard a sharp intake of breath at the other end that ended with a gurgling sound. It was a combination of a wail and a sob.

'You there, Tony?' he asked.

'Fucking Mathur!' Tony was shouting at the other end.

'Who's Mathur?' Dippy asked.

'Amit Mathur. The mother-fucker. He's one of my best friends!' Tony's voice was a high-pitched scream now.

'Calm down, Tony,' Dippy said.

'He's the closest friend I have,' wailed Tony. 'A mole on the cheek and a limp. Parktown. I've always had a nagging doubt. My God, I've been betrayed.'

'Easy, my friend,' Dippy tried to calm the man down. 'Let's meet right now and discuss the next move.'

'I have to go now.' Tony's voice was suddenly calm.

Dippy had a dreadful feeling in the pit of his stomach. 'Wait. Don't go anywhere,' he pleaded. 'Come to my office first so we can work out a plan of action.'

The line had already gone dead. Dippy staggered over to a timber tallboy next to his desk and poured a drink. There was nothing more that he could have done.

Dippy heard the news on the morning TV broadcast at home. Much of what was reported was also splashed across the front page of every local newspaper.

Man apprehended after stabbing friend at
Parktown – for no apparent reason.

The police had arrested a man named Tony Vaz at the house of his friend Amit Mathur in Parktown. Vaz had stabbed Mathur several times in the chest and death had been instantaneous. The police and the neighbours had no idea about the motive behind the vicious attack. It was also reported that Vaz was in a state of extreme intoxication at the time of his arrest and that he refused to speak to anyone.

Dippy Singh switched off the television, walked over to the telephone and then dialled a number.

A crisp female voice answered at the other end.

'It's me,' Dippy said. 'Did you see the morning news?'

'Hi, darling,' Cheryl said. 'Yes, I did. It seems to have worked.'

'Yes,' replied Dippy. There was a ghost of a smile on his lips and a faraway look in his eyes. 'It was just a matter of chance that he picked my name from the Yellow Pages and the rest was just...well, lateral thinking, I guess.'

All in the Family

Gurdas Singh pulled up a chair and sank in comfortably at a small table in a quiet corner of the Trinity Café. It was the fall of 1957 and a particularly cloudy morning in Miami. The quiet corner allowed him to focus on his studies, away from the vociferous conversations of countless students who frequented the cafe. Trinity Café was close to the University of Miami, where he was a postgraduate student in the department of atmospheric sciences. The hangout was particularly popular among the university students, more for the reasonable prices than the quality.

It was during his second cup of cappuccino that he saw a shadow fall across his books on the table. He looked up and was a little surprised to see a girl smiling down at him. She was a pretty brunette with blue eyes and a very prominent slant of the eyebrows. She looked vaguely familiar.

He returned her smile with a soft 'Hi.'

'Hey,' replied the brunette extending her hand for a cordial handshake. 'I'm Jennifer Ryan. I think we often pass each other in the department corridors and I thought I might as well catch up with you.'

He remembered that he had often seen her between classes and had on many occasions exchanged courteous nods.

'Is this a good time to catch up?' Jennifer asked, looking down at the mound of books on the table.

'Not a problem at all,' Gurdas said. 'Please pull up a chair. Can I order a coffee for you?'

It was the beginning of a long friendship that converted inevitably into courtship after four years. However, the migration from courtship to marriage proposal took two more years since academia took priority over romance. Ironically, Gurdas finally proposed to Jennifer at the Trinity Café over a cup of the perennial cappuccino and at the same table where they had first met.

After that, he was quick to make a call to his parents in India about the good tidings. However, to his dismay, his long-winded romance hit a brick wall when his family refused to accept his decision to marry an American girl. He hailed from a small village in Punjab, where marrying outside the family caste was akin to blasphemy. After countless conversations that often ended in heated exchanges or tearful beseeches, he bowed to the pressure from his family. The final nail in the argument was hammered in when, during a conversation with his mother, she insinuated that she would rather take her own life than tell society that her son had married an American.

The biggest dilemma was, of course, Jennifer; and he spent many sleepless nights trying to figure out a way of telling her about his predicament. On several occasions, he even mustered up courage to discuss the matter with her but was simply unable to do so at the very last moment. Over the next few painful days, he came to a conclusion that he would never be able to tell Jennifer about his decision. He started his preparations for the trip to India and then told Jennifer that he needed to get back to India quickly since his mother had been struck down with a serious illness.

On a warm morning in the month of April 1963, Gurdas left for India.

Once he reached his village, Gurdas's parents did not waste any time in getting him married to a local girl by the name of Harjit Kaur. Unknown to him, the marriage had been finalised nearly three years ago. The girl was from a traditional Sikh family and brought up with the necessary skills needed to manage a household and look after a family, as is often the case in many Indian families. The hullabaloo of the wedding was contagious and swept Gurdas off his feet for a few days. Once the celebrations had died down, Gurdas wrote a very long letter to Jennifer informing about his situation, albeit with profuse apologies and sadness. He did not expect a reply and he did not get one.

Within the next few months, he started preparing for his return to the United States. He applied for a PhD program at various universities, making sure that they were far away from Florida. Gurdas had a brilliant academic track record and his application to Michigan Tech was quickly accepted. Within a couple of weeks, he was on a flight to Michigan. Once there, Gurdas immediately filed the migration documents for Harjit and then immersed himself in his studies, with all his spare time devoted to setting up a neat home for his wife.

Life got even more demanding for Gurdas after the arrival of Harjit Kaur and, between work and domestic duties, the years started flying by quickly. Within three years, he completed his doctorate and was offered an excellent position at a local research company.

However, Harjit was not a happy soul in Michigan. Lacking the accepted social skills, she hardly had any friends and felt socially isolated. She had a lonely life during the day and could hardly go anywhere on her own, having stubbornly refused to improve her driving skills. Driven by this self-inflicted misery, she implored Gurdas to apply for migration to Australia, where she had two cousins in Melbourne.

When Gurdas showed his unwillingness to agree to her proposal, she argued that she would have a much fuller life in Australia and far better social conditions since they would be able to live within an extended family. Gurdas was not very keen on moving to Australia, but he was a rational man who knew the values of a happy household. After making a few inquiries about his prospects in Melbourne, he decided to give it a try. In the worst case, he said to himself, he could always come back.

Life in Melbourne turned out to be much better than Gurdas expected and he quite enjoyed the extended family that he now had. More than anything else, the weather suited him very well. Getting a good job was never an issue for him and he readily accepted a senior position at the Institute of Sciences in Melbourne.

Over the next few years, Gurdas became the proud recipient of many research grants and prestigious awards that added to his already formidable reputation as a scientist. On the home front, things got happier with the advent of the twins, a boy and a girl who were named Inder Singh and Amandeep Kaur. Although challenging at times, he was quite happy to divide his time and attention between home and the growing pressures at work.

After taking up Australian permanent residency, Gurdas and Harjit started living the great Australian dream. They built a beautiful house in a decent Melbourne suburb and the kids grew up into diligent and responsible teenagers. Academically, they seemed to take after their father. Both excelled at school and university and then took up academic careers at Melbourne University.

Thirty years passed by. For Gurdas, the years felt like thirty days. In those three decades, he felt that he had achieved all he had set out to do in life. On the professional front, his excellence in research was heralded not only by the Indian diaspora in Melbourne but also by the Australian press. He rose to the position of director at the institute and was nominated to the boards of many prestigious national and international organisations. Excellence in work also brought financial prosperity and on the home front, he could not have asked for anything better.

Harjit had acquired a social status that suited her well. She revelled in the glory of her family. Her extended family, which had grown to a very large size, looked up to her.

However, as is often the case, what lurks around the corners in life is hard to predict at the best of times and in the fall of the year 1999, Harjit was diagnosed with pulmonary fibrosis – an irreversible disease of the lungs. After numerous consultations with local GPs and specialists, the fatality of the situation became very apparent to Gurdas. In the end, he decided to retire from work and devote his time looking after Harjit and he wasted no time in tendering his resignation.

The next five years, as he had expected, were possibly the hardest for him and the family. Harjit's condition got worse with each year and it got to the point where she could hardly move or talk without acute distress. In those months, endurance reached breaking point for Gurdas and often, when he was alone, he found himself praying for her peaceful demise.

On a cold Melbourne morning, five years after she was diagnosed with the fatal disease, Harjit Kaur passed away peacefully, surrounded by her family and many members of her extended one.

After Harjit's death, Gurdas became an unwilling social recluse, immersing himself in his books and journals. He rarely went out and, in spite of repeated persuasions from his children, he refrained from meeting people or going to social functions. He would probably have spent the rest of his life in that fashion had he not received a letter of invitation to a seminar in Miami.

He was quite surprised that he had been specially invited by his old alma mater and was thrilled that he had been asked to give a presentation at an internationally known conference. The letter also brought back many memories of his days in Miami and of course, his time with Jennifer. The reminiscences seemed far away and the memories were like a vision through a mist. It had been three years since his wife's death and he was quite determined to attend the conference. He also felt that the trip might be a good change, away from home and his books, and very soon he became engrossed in preparations for his trip to Miami. All this, of course, made his children quite happy, as they were starting to worry about his mental well-being.

The trip to Miami turned out to be even better than Gurdas had expected, because he managed to get in touch with many of his old friends and acquaintances. On most evenings after the daytime seminars, he was invited to dinner by his friends and he got to visit many places that he had frequented during his early years in the city. However, he carefully avoided asking about Jennifer and he was quite surprised that none of them even brought her name up, given the fact that most of them knew about his relationship with her and the ensuing events.

His trip was only for a couple of weeks and on the day before his departure, his friends decided to host a dinner to see him off. To his immense pleasure and surprise, the venue they selected was the Trinity Café where he had passed countless evenings as a student.

On the day of the farewell, Gurdas arrived at the café and was surprised to see that place was no longer the little café that he frequented in the fifties. It had transformed itself into a gorgeous restaurant under a new management and looked stunning. He was warmly greeted outside by Trilok Singh, his closest ally since his college days, and one who had been instrumental in organising the special dinner.

'Do you recognise the place, my friend?' Trilok asked, having observed the look in Gurdas's eyes.

'Of course,' Gurdas replied. 'And it does bring back many memories.'

'Anything in particular?' There was a twinkle in Trilok's eyes.

Gurdas nodded. There was a faraway look in his eyes.

'Jennifer?' Trilok asked.

'Yes… I wonder where she is now.'

Trilok smiled at Gurdas. 'Well, not very far, to be honest,' he said.

'What do you mean?'

'She's waiting for us in the café, Gurdas,'

Gurdas shook his head in protest. He felt embarrassed.

'Hey,' Trilok said, 'she was in the audience during your presentation at the conference and she specially asked me to invite her to the send-off dinner. It was something that I could hardly refuse, my friend.'

Gurdas was quite shaken up by then and could hardly speak. He just kept on shaking his head.

'Come on, Gurdas.' Trilok put an arm around Gurdas's shoulder. 'It's been decades now. We're all stepping into the twilight of our lives. It's time to meet, greet and forget the discrepancies of life. She's very eager to see you.'

Gurdas found himself being slowly shoved towards the entrance door and his legs felt laden with lead. The table had been set up at the end of the café in a brightly lit corner. Most of the décor had changed, but Gurdas still remembered the surroundings. As they entered, everyone round the table stood up with smiles and greetings. Gurdas managed to put on a brave smile and looked around the table with growing trepidation, till his eyes came to rest upon a dapper lady who stood at the back of the crowd, a disarming smile on her face. It was Jennifer. The brunette hair was white now and her face was etched with wrinkles. However, the bright blue eyes and the slanting eyebrows were a giveaway. Gurdas shook hands with everyone till he stood in front of Jennifer. She probably saw the slight hesitation, because she stepped forward and gave him a big hug. Gurdas felt a little uncomfortable at first, but the smiles around him soon put him at ease.

The guests settled in amidst the plentiful food and drinks and, very soon, Gurdas found himself chatting with everyone. There were many stories to share and recount.

Time flew by and before long it was time to leave. Gurdas went through the warm handshakes and tearful hugs as the guests left. Finally, he was left alone with Jennifer. He sensed that she was a little hesitant to leave.

'Do you want another drink before you leave?' he asked. 'A small nightcap perhaps?'

She nodded.

Gurdas felt a tap on his shoulder. It was Trilok.

'I'll pick you up at six a.m. tomorrow. Your flight leaves at nine. Don't be late,' Trilok said with a mischievous twinkle in his eyes.

In spite of the guarded hint, Gurdas and Jennifer spent the next three hours together. The first hour was spent at the café and the rest at a local diner. They talked incessantly. They spoke about the days gone by and discussed their current lives: the trials, the tribulations, the jubilant moments and the sad times. As they summarised their lives, Gurdas felt as if they had separated only a few days ago. She recounted, how after their separation, she had married a professor at the university, a kind gentleman by the name of David Browne, and settled down in Miami. She had inquired about Gurdas from mutual friends and, for some time, had even followed his professional life with great interest. With the passing years, she had stopped inquiring, especially after the birth of her daughter. She recounted how satisfying her life had been with her family and how that happiness had come to an abrupt end with the unexpected death of her husband. As the two long-lost friends exchanged their life stories, time seemed to fly by seamlessly.

Suddenly Gurdas realised that it was well past midnight and he had an early flight to catch. In the last three hours, a glimmer of hope had shone on his lonely life and he wondered if he should ask the question that lurked in the recesses of his mind. In the end, he managed to muster up enough courage. 'Jennifer,' he said. 'I have an early flight tomorrow.'

Jennifer looked at him and smiled. 'Time to part?'

'Yes, I guess,' Gurdas replied, looking away. 'However, I still have a question for you.'

'Sure.'

A short silence ensued and then Gurdas looked at her with an apologetic cough. 'I don't know how to say this,' he said. 'I just wanted to know if there was any hope for us to rekindle our lives together. I think a sense of loneliness has permeated our lives.'

He could see traces of a blush spreading across Jennifer's face. She looked away for a few moments. Moments that felt like years.

'It's really nice of you to say that,' she said at last. 'I'll need to think about it.'

Gurdas smiled. 'Of course,' he said. 'It's a big decision for both of us. Maybe you can come to Melbourne for a short visit and we can take it further.' Gurdas noticed a slight twinkle in the blue eyes.

'I didn't tell you about this,' Jennifer said, 'but there is a strong reason for me to come to Melbourne. My daughter works at a company there.'

Gurdas could scarcely believe his ears. 'Goodness gracious!' he exclaimed. 'What an extraordinary coincidence. Well, it's decided then! You must come to Melbourne. See the city and visit your daughter as well. That will give us enough time to think about our future.'

Jennifer thought for a while and said, 'Yes, that sounds great. But I'll wait for your call.'

Gurdas looked at her kindly. 'You won't need to wait long, I promise you.'

The couple parted after a couple of hugs that were a little more than just warm farewell gestures.

Gurdas returned to Melbourne and felt that he was a changed man. There was a sparkle in his tired eyes and a slight spring in his steps. He decided to first contemplate on the new events in his life before making the final decision and informing his children.

The next few days were hard for Gurdas as his mind swirled with countless questions and thoughts. It took him nearly a week to make the final decision: he was convinced that he did want to get Jennifer over to Melbourne and if possible settle down with her for the rest of his life. Since it was usual for his son to join him for dinner every Sunday, he thought that it would be an opportune moment to break the news to his son at the next Sunday dinner. He could then call Jennifer to tell her about his decision.

On Sunday evening, Gurdas ordered some takeaway dinner from the local Indian restaurant and chilled a bottle of champagne that he had been saving for a special occasion. And this was indeed a very special moment for him. Although he felt a slight trepidation about Inder's reaction, he was quite comfortable with his decision and he knew that the support of his children would be strong as always. He felt excited but a little apprehensive as he waited anxiously for Inder.

The doorbell and the clock nearly chimed simultaneously at seven p.m. and Gurdas hurried to the front door, more eager than usual. He wrenched open the door and was a little startled to see Inder standing there with his arm around a demure Caucasian girl. She was desperately trying to put on a brave smile. Overcoming his surprise, Gurdas put on a smile and beckoned the couple inside.

Inder was his usual relaxed self. 'You look pretty surprised, Dad,' he said.

'Not really,' Gurdas lied. 'It's just that I was expecting to see you alone.'

The girl shifted uncomfortably on her feet.

'This is Irene, Dad,' said Inder and after a slight pause, he added, 'And I have some good news for you.'

Gurdas sensed what was coming. He shook hands with Irene.

'Sorry to do this to you so suddenly, Dad,' Inder continued. 'But I thought I must introduce you to Irene today. More so, because I proposed to her yesterday.'

'That's excellent news!' Gurdas exclaimed. 'Although I must confess that this is a bit of a surprise. I had no inkling at all.'

'We wanted to keep this under wraps,' said the young lady. The American drawl was unmistakable. 'You are the first person to know about it.'

Gurdas nodded and smiled back at Irene. 'Come in, please. I think I need to pop a special bottle of champagne today.' He walked towards the kitchen. 'Celebrations are in order, I think.'

In the kitchen, Gurdas smiled to himself as he poured the drinks. Inder was marrying an American girl! Another American in the family.

Gurdas carried the drinks into the living room. Inder and Irene had made themselves comfortable on the overstuffed sofa. Might not be the right moment to speak to them about Jennifer, Gurdas thought. Maybe another day.

As he put down the tray on the table, Irene looked around.

'Do you need some help in the kitchen?' she asked, getting up.

It was possibly the combination of her blue eyes, the slanted eyebrows and the slight tilt of the head to one side that brought a quick flashback of a face to Gurdas.

He stared at Irene for a few moments. 'You remind me of a very close friend in Miami,' he said.

Irene stood up with a smile. 'Really? I'm from Miami myself.'

Gurdas paused momentarily as he felt a sense of foreboding. 'That's interesting,' he said. 'You quite remind me of an old friend from my university days. Jennifer Ryan.'

Irene had a look of incredulity written all over her face. She let out a husky nervous laugh and looked at Inder. 'This is unbelievable,' she cried out. She turned towards Gurdas. 'Do you mean Jennifer Browne? My mother's maiden name was Jennifer Ryan.'

'Yes, of course,' said Gurdas trying to sound very excited. 'It's Jennifer Browne that I refer to. We were great friends during our university days and just met up in Miami, after decades.'

'This is an unbelievable coincidence,' said Inder, walking up to Irene and putting his arm around her.

'It is indeed an extraordinary coincidence,' said Gurdas, his eyes clouding over. 'Now… Who would have thought? Life is indeed full of surprises, isn't it?'

While the excited couple hugged each other in a show of joy and astonishment, Gurdas did not wait for an answer to his question. He just walked slowly to the kitchen to set out dinner. It was just as well since he did not want Inder to catch a glimpse of the look on his face; a look of disappointment and surprise.

Inder married Irene after three months.

Gurdas never made that promised phone call to Jennifer and he was not surprised when Jennifer excused herself from the wedding saying that she was too unwell to travel.

The Other Flag

It was a cold morning in June when Vikas Khanna stepped off a plane and walked into Sydney airport. He could feel a strange mix of apprehension and excitement. He was not sure if it was happiness or a deep down feeling of sadness because his entry into the warm airport was the culmination of years of planning, divisive arguments, heartaches, and anxiety. The year was 2008.

Vikas was from a small town called Ramnivas, eighty kilometres south of New Delhi in India. Brought up in a middle-class family, he was part of the constant middle-class feud that had bisected the country into two distinct classes. He had completed his graduation but had found no solace in the fact that his qualification might take him nowhere in the real world of employment. At the same time, many of friends who had managed to settle overseas brought back stories that had fuelled his imagination and boosted his urge to go to these foreign lands that promised so much prosperity and gratification.

During a trip to Delhi in 2008, he had chanced upon a reliable agent who was offering facilities for students to migrate to Australia. Vikas had returned home with copies of migration papers and other necessary forms. He was not surprised when his enthusiastic excitement was met with damp caution at home and even subtle disapproval from his parents. During that period, India was rife with rumours about the violence against Indian students in Sydney and Melbourne. After his return, Vikas had spent the next few days arguing his case with his parents. Voices were regularly raised, and discussions often ended with angry words from his father or his mother's quiet tears.

However, Vikas had always been convinced that his fortunes lay elsewhere; in a foreign land like Australia. What added strength to his intent was the fact that his close friend Sanjay Vatsal had settled happily in Sydney, landing there a couple of years ago on a student visa, and had found a lot of comfort in his studies and part-time jobs. Since that time, unknown to his parents, Vikas had also nurtured a secret desire to move overseas and had made a conscious decision to leave India for good. Although his family had never been in any stage of impoverishment, he was quite tired of the constant rush, the unsatisfied needs and the never-ending pressures of society that India enforced on the surging middle class.

In spite of the forewarnings and concerns from his parents, Vikas had then applied for a student's visa and, in a few months' time, had set sail for Australia, the land of plentiful promises.

As Vikas stepped out of Sydney airport, his heart swelled with expectations and Sydney, in turn, did not let him down. He fell in love with the city. He shared his lodgings with Sanjay Vatsal, took a liking to his studies, found work at a local restaurant and even started saving a little money (thanks to the quiet discretion of the restaurant owner who offered him more than the legal twenty hours of work that he was allowed as a student). Although he had little leisurely time on hand, Vikas managed to build up a good circle of Indian friends. To his absolute delight, this closed circle of friends also had a few very nice-looking Punjabi girls.

Yes, life felt good. That is, until the first incident.

It happened towards the fall of 2008, in the month of November during a quiet warm night right in the heart of Harris Park and very close to the apartment where Vikas lived. His first source of information was the television and then the morning news. Both screamed about the attack on an Indian student on a street in Harris Park. Upon hearing the morning news, Vikas rushed back into the bedroom and woke up Sanjay from his slumber. The two of them then huddled together in front of the television set listening to the news about the violent attack. Immediately after that, they called their friends, only to find that the news had already spread through the student community the night before.

Vikas spent the next few anxious days with friends and the discussions hardly deviated from this single issue. Stories about racial vilification, that had never been revealed before, came from all those who had been targeted in the past. Rampant stories of violence against ethnic classes started to proliferate among the Indians in Sydney, especially within the student communities. Tales of distress soon gave way to anger and it was decided by the students that some action needed to be taken. A body of students was then formed, headed by a few self-proclaimed leaders of the community who, as was usually the case, had come out of the woodwork.

Vikas joined this movement wholeheartedly. He started spending the evenings with different groups, all with the single-minded objective of fighting against the racial vilification that had turned so violent. He was a proud member of a select group who led a procession to the state parliament house and were later invited to express their concerns at a meeting with a local member of the parliament. Vikas felt delighted about his activities and his involvement with the protest groups was widely lauded by his friends. He had never felt so patriotic in his life and had never felt so much love for his motherland India.

Things really turned sour for Vikas when, a few weeks later, he had a first-hand experience during a short trip to the local supermarket. It was a warm Sunday and as he strolled down the road towards the shops, he came upon a group of Middle Eastern youths standing outside a local bottle shop. Before he could circumvent the group, he was shoved by a young muscular man. Vikas quickly crossed over to the other side of the road amidst jibes and jeers. As he hurried away, he heard one them yell out, 'Bloody Indian. Go back to where you came from!'

Vikas was too scared to look back at the group as he hastened towards his apartment. For the very first time, he felt humiliated in Australia. He felt like a lost soul in an alienated world. He had faced many crises in life, but this blatant insult brought back memories of home. He yearned for the calming voice of his father and the coaxing arm of his mother. That night, Vikas wondered what made him come to a country where he never belonged, and his fear and humiliation were soon replaced with anger. He was surprised at the amount of loathing that filled his heart. That very night, he decided to take a break from his studies and go back to his hometown in India. He felt that he needed to think about his future and had a pressing urge to find out where he really belonged.

Within four weeks, he was back in Ramnivas, where he was greeted with the kind of jubilation that one usually associates with festivities. He was soon spoilt rotten by his parents and friends. Everyone wanted to hear good stories from Australia but all Vikas wanted to recount were stories of racism, violence and hatred for Indian students. To his dismay, his father even reminded him about the warnings that he never heeded before he left for Australia. He felt that he had lost his way in life and, within his heart, he placed the blame squarely at the doorstep of Australia.

It was just the fifth day at home when Vikas heard rumours that a student rally was being organised in New Delhi to protest against the violence in Australia. He quickly made a few phone calls to confirm the date of the rally and was soon on his way to New Delhi. He felt that it was his moral duty to join the rally and his heart filled with excitement at the thought of his participation. He had never felt so proud to be an Indian.

The rally that was deemed to be peaceful turned quite ugly as students gave vent to their pent-up anger against the country that had marred their ambitions amidst claims of racism and violence. The air was rife with vociferous slogans of 'Long live India' and 'Death to racism in Australia'. Suddenly, someone produced an Australian flag and a few stentorian voices called for the flag to be burnt. When Vikas saw the slight hesitation within the crowd, he stepped forward and lit a match. A roar of appreciation went up around him. He nearly fainted with the patriotism that welled up in his heart. Proudly, he picked up the Australian flag and set it on fire. The police immediately swooped down on the crowd and dispersed the protesters within a matter of minutes. Vikas, however, came out of the rally with a feeling of successful retribution.

Vikas wanted to spend a few more days in Delhi but hastened back home after getting the news that his father had met with an accident. After returning, he immediately took his father to the local GP, who ordered an immediate scan. The scans revealed that there was severe damage to the lungs. This meant that he needed to be transported to New Delhi for an immediate operation. Vikas, however, needed to follow up with the police about the accident since his father had been struck down by a speeding car that had apparently lost control. He landed up at the local police station a day later.

The constable in charge of the station came to the point very quickly. 'Sir, you know it is quite hard to get these papers processed. A little money might speed up matters,' he said.

'And how much would that be?' Vikas asked. He could hardly believe his ears.

The constable's eyes shifted around. 'Three thousand should be enough,' he said.

Vikas stood up abruptly. He was outraged. 'Three thousand rupees?' he asked. 'But my father is the victim here, not the criminal.'

'Sahib,' said the constable with a slimy smile, 'the car was being driven by Kumar Saini. I am sure you have heard of him.'

Vikas had indeed heard stories about Kumar Saini. The son of the richest landlord in town, Kumar's name was mentioned in hushed whispers and his connection with the underworld was well-known. Vikas remained unmoved. 'What if I do pay the money? Can you assure me that I can then lodge a complaint against this man?' he asked.

The constable's eyes shifted away. 'The money is for my protection, sahib,' he said. 'You can pay now and come back tomorrow to register the case. I need to take care of a few things related to the case before you lodge your complaint.'

Vikas stared at him. He found it very hard to trust this man.

'Everything will be taken care of,' the constable added, as an afterthought. 'Just ask for me. My name is Mulayam Singh.'

'Please make sure that I can register the complaint tomorrow,' Vikas said, fishing into his shoulder bag for his wallet. 'I need to take my father to Delhi for an urgent operation.'

The cash was quickly counted and handed over. The constable surreptitiously pocketed the booty and then stood up, indicating the end of the discussion. Vikas retreated slowly and with a very heavy heart.

He went back to the police station very early next day and, to his surprise, he was met by a different officer inside. The constable, who was in the midst of having tea with a well-dressed young man, looked up with a sneer as Vikas entered the room. Vikas introduced himself and recounted the incident.

'Aah,' said the new constable stretching his arms, 'Constable Mulayam Singh was here yesterday on temporary deputation. He has now gone back to another police station.'

Vikas raised his hands in protest and dropped his voice to a whisper as he leaned towards the officer. 'I paid him some cash for my case,' he hissed.

The officer looked at him nonchalantly. 'You should not have paid him, my friend. Bribes are not allowed at this station. I can't help you.'

Vikas looked on dumbfounded, his face suffused with blood and he could no longer contain his anger. 'You will have to resolve this issue,' he said, pointing a finger at the officer, 'unless you want me to complain to higher authorities in the police department.'

The officer stood up defiantly. He pointed towards the young man, who had so far silently watched the unfolding scene. 'Do you know who this is, my friend?' he asked. 'This is Kumar Saini. I don't think he needs any further introduction and I would strongly recommend that you leave immediately.'

Vikas looked closely at Kumar Saini. The young man stared back with an ingratiating smile on his face. Behind that smile, however, was a pair of stony eyes that froze Vikas. He felt helpless and it dawned upon him quickly that this was a battle he could never win. He got up and walked out of the room slowly. The deathly silence behind him stopped him from looking back. Once outside, he could hardly breathe. He just staggered to a bench on the roadside and stared into space. He was not worried about the money. What caused the pain was the helplessness that he felt and his inability to appeal to justice for his injured father.

Vikas realised that he could no longer wait and that he needed to rush his father to Delhi for the operation and the only way to do so was to hire a car. He rang up his friend Rajkumar in Delhi and asked him to book a room for his father in a privately owned hospital that was recommended by his local GP. Rajkumar called back within an hour to say that the hospital was full and the only way of getting in was to bribe the booking clerk. Eight thousand rupees had to be handed over as a 'token gift' for admission and another twenty-five thousand rupees towards the surgeon's 'booking' fees for the operation. Vikas, who had surrendered to the system by then, asked Rajkumar to pay whatever was necessary to get his father admitted.

Within the next hour, Vikas was on his way to Delhi with his father, in a private car. Albeit, once the driver of the car realised the urgency of the situation, he charged Vikas nearly double the hiring charges. Giving in to the rules of a corrupt society was the only salvation for Vikas and he was quite happy to grease every palm along the way as long as his father received the urgent medical care that he needed.

Vikas reached Delhi in the early hours of a misty morning and headed straight for the hospital. The state of his father's health weighed heavily on his mind as he was met by his friend Rajkumar at the entrance of the hospital. To his dismay, the clerk at the reception desk informed him that there would be a waiting time of more than six hours. Vikas's fury knew no bounds and he decided to fight for his case with alacrity and vehemence. His father needed immediate attention and he knew that he was running out of time.

Rajkumar held him back. 'It's pointless arguing your case, Vikas,' he said. 'You have no option but to bide your time. We have no proof of the money that has been paid. Out here, monetary transactions and bribes are all based on trust. If you want your work done, you need to trust the clerk who took the money.'

Vikas sat down next to his father, holding his head in his hands. He looked up as he felt his father's hand on his shoulders. Vikas saw the hunted look in his father's eyes.

His father smiled at him. 'This is India, Vikas. Here, who you are and who you know is all that matters. You have to be very patient in this country, my son. Things do not work the way they do in other countries.' His voiced trailed away as he winced in pain.

Vikas could only look on in dismay. He felt defeated and confused and the next six hours were the longest that he had ever faced. The state of his father's health worsened with every hour and his father's groans brought tears into his eyes. By the end of the fourth hour, he had to make his father lie down on one of the bedraggled sofas. The pain was getting unbearable for the old man. Unable to control his anxiety, Vikas finally walked up to the reception desk and requested someone to do a check on his father.

'Do you think we're sitting around idling away our time, sir?' the clerk snarled.

'But he is in a lot of pain,' said Vikas. 'At least give him some painkillers.'

'This is not a house of charity, my friend,' the clerk replied. 'You can buy him some analgesic tablets from the pharmacy outside.'

Vikas immediately got Rajkumar to buy some tablets from the shop outside. However, the medicine could hardly contain the pain. Vikas looked around desperately, clutching his father's arm. It somehow reminded him of a visit to a zoo when he was a child, when he had held his father's hand in fear. Tears welled up in his eyes.

However, within the next hour, to his surprise, Vikas was summoned to the front desk. He walked up to the clerk with a slight glimmer of hope in his heart.

'We have spoken to the surgeon, sir,' said the clerk. 'Since this needs to be done in an emergency, the fees need to be slightly more.'

'How much would that be?' asked Vikas.

'Four hundred thousand rupees is the best that the surgeon can do.'

'Four hundred thousand?' asked Vikas. There was a look of stunned disbelief on his face. 'How can I get that kind of money? I'm just an ordinary man.'

The clerk looked away. 'But this is not an ordinary operation, sir. Your father looks very ill and needs immediate attention from the doctor.'

'But I really cannot afford that amount. Please have some pity on the man. Please.'

The clerk stared at him. 'I cannot spend any more time with you, sir,' he said. 'If you really cannot afford the money, then you need to look elsewhere.'

Vikas could hardly believe his ears. He opened his mouth in protest, but the clerk had already turned away towards others who were waiting around the busy desk. Vikas looked helplessly at Rajkumar and said in a voice that was hardly audible, 'Where do we go now?'

The next two days seemed like two years to Vikas. He kept his father at Rajkumar's little apartment and ran from one hospital to another begging for his father's health. The evenings were spent ringing up his local friends and family members for financial help. A local GP was brought in by Rajkumar, which hardly mattered because the old man was sinking quickly. On the third day, Rajkumar managed to find a surgeon who was ready to do the operation for much less. But it was all too late. His father passed away that very day.

With some much-needed help from Rajkumar, Vikas organised the funeral for his father in New Delhi itself, since he found it extremely hard to transfer his father's body to Ramnivas. His grieving family was transported to Delhi quickly, thanks to a taxi driver known to the family. It proved to be two of the most harrowing days in Vikas's life. The inconsolable family, the social pressures, the red tape, the corruption and diminishing funds ate into his soul as never before. He was therefore not surprised when he felt a yearning for Australia and, in spite of his family's pleas to him to return with them, he decided to catch a flight to Australia at the earliest opportunity.

He stayed with his family at Rajkumar's apartment for three days before managing to book a flight back to Sydney. Before he left, he made the final arrangements for his family's return to Ramnivas and when he finally boarded the flight there were strange feelings within his heart that vied for attention: sadness and desolation combined with a distinct glimmer of relief.

It was a very warm morning when he landed in Sydney. Once he reached his apartment, he got into his bed without even changing his clothes. He spent a few hours recalling the terrible events of the past few days, tossing and turning, finding the events almost surreal. He soon fell asleep, exhausted, and woke up with a start as a loud ambulance passed on the street below. It was completely dark and he realised that he had slept through the entire day. He looked at his watch. It was past eight in the evening.

Vikas got up and staggered into the small kitchen and pulled a chair towards a ramshackle cupboard where he stored some of his old belongings. He stood up on the chair, tottering slightly with the grogginess, reached deep into the top shelf and pulled out a small Indian flag that he had brought with him when he had first landed in Australia.

Then, he quietly walked down the stairs and into the overgrown backyard. He looked around to ensure that he was alone and then placed the flag neatly on the ground. He knelt down, carefully produced a matchbox from his pocket and meticulously set the flag on fire. After that, he just sat there quietly, watching the flag burn amidst chirping crickets, till the embers died down.

The Inheritance

Ranjit Pal sipped on his morning cup of tea and looked out of the window. He could hear the birds chirping and some kids playing in the neighbour's yard. On another day, he would have quite enjoyed these happy sounds. However, he remained lost in thought with a bemused expression on his face. Since his retirement early in the year, he had been constantly dogged by questions about his superannuation savings. For most retirees in Australia, this was a no-brainer. People usually would have the money in the superannuation fund invested in stocks, bonds and, for the wealthier, in real estate. Superannuation was the nest egg for every Australian; a hope for the future.

Ranjit Pal was, however, in a more complex situation. He had spent his years in Australia as a science teacher in schools; a career that had given him more satisfaction than money. But he had always lived within his means. He had a small house in the suburb of Liverpool in Sydney, a caring wife and a son. Life had been very uneventful and completely devoid of excitement. Yet it had been a satisfying life. Since the time he migrated from India thirty-five years ago, he had never travelled outside Australia except for his visits back home to the city of Calcutta. The upside of this frugal lifestyle was that he had been able to save more into his retirement fund. He often proclaimed proudly among friends that he had managed to put away a tidy sum for his future. It was his only hope for a comfortable life in the years ahead.

But now he was faced with a conundrum. Back in Calcutta, he had grown up in a household where it was the tradition for the father to provide a degree of care for the children. His grandfather had left a little house for his father. His father, in turn, had left Ranjit a small monetary inheritance. Since Ranjit had three siblings, his inheritance was not a sizeable one but enough to see him through his university studies. When his son, Ajoy, was born in Australia, Ranjit had pledged that he would leave some pecuniary inheritance for his son. It was a matter of pride and duty for him.

Ranjit's wish had become a necessity when he had recognised that Ajoy was not a bright child. At school, Ajoy could only get mediocre grades. After that, he had barely managed to get through an accounting course in one of the lesser known TAFE colleges. On the completion of his accounting studies, Ajoy had managed to get a clerical job in a small firm. Ranjit had soon come to the conclusion that his son was a diligent, hard-working individual but hardly someone who would make a fortune out of his career. This had strengthened Ranjit's resolution to help his son in whatever way possible.

Ranjit put down his cup and looked up as his wife Lolita came in with the customary plate of toast and jam. Ranjit decided to confer immediately with his wife about the matter weighing on his mind. After listening to Ranjit's wish of transferring some money to Ajoy's name, Lolita advised him to first discuss the matter with his close friends. Later in the day, he called his close friends and debated his option of withdrawing a lump sum from his superannuation fund in order to bequeath his son some money. However, to his dismay, he found that most of the opinions his friends offered him differed from his own. Unable to come to a conclusion, he finally decided to take advice from Ramdas Roy, his closest friend and confidant. He had known Ramdas all his life and, on many occasions, advice from the astute gentleman had helped Ranjit to make important decisions in life. Without further delay, Ranjit went to meet Ramdas at his home.

To his surprise, even Ramdas's advice was quite contrary to Ranjit's intentions.

'Tread with care, Ranjit,' Ramdas told him. 'Please do not give away money that you have saved for your future.'

Ranjit tried arguing his case. 'But I want to do something for my son. He does not have a bright future. I need to give him the money when he needs it the most.'

Ramdas shook his head. 'Do not get into a position where you are not the master of your wealth. It's great to help the children but never at the cost of your own financial independence. It can have severe repercussions.'

Ranjit was severely disappointed. He returned home in a thoughtful mood. Why can't I help my son? My father helped me when I needed it the most. I cannot let this happen.

He spent the next few days discussing the matter with his wife. After weighing the available options, they decided to keep some money for themselves and give the rest to Ajoy so that he could buy a decent house. In the next few days, Ranjit and Lolita found an opportune moment to discuss the details of their plan with Ajoy.

They sat around the dining table and Ranjit laid out his strategy for the future. 'Ajoy,' he said. 'I have now retired from active work and, following in my father's footsteps, I think that I need to do something for you.'

Ajoy looked on silently. He could not fathom the course the discussion was taking.

Ranjit continued with his soliloquy. 'Your mother and I have decided to set you up with a contribution from my super fund account. I want to withdraw a lump sum from my superannuation fund and sell this house. We will then have enough money to buy a bigger house in a better suburb, where we can all live together. The new house will be in your name.'

Ajoy stared speechlessly at his parents for a few moments. 'That is extremely generous of you, Dad,' he said at last. 'But I can't let you do it. This is your money, your savings for your future.'

Ranjit smiled at his son. 'My father helped me when I was young. It is important for me to carry on this tradition.'

Ajoy shook his head. 'How will you manage your day-to-day expenses? My salary is not enough to support three of us.'

Lolita spoke for the first time. 'Your dad has decided to only withdraw a chunk of his super fund,' she said. 'We will still have enough money for our daily expenses.'

'And don't forget that I will be starting private tuition very soon,' Ranjit interjected. 'That will add to the family income. I think we will do well.'

Ajoy looked down for a moment. When he spoke, his voice was hardly more than a whisper. 'I wish I had a lucrative career. Then I could have looked after the two of you without all this.'

Ranjit smiled benignly at his son. 'This is my duty, son,' he said. 'I am doing this with a lot of pride and joy.'

In the next few days, Ranjit set his plan in motion. He organised the necessary paperwork to withdraw money from his superannuation fund and started looking for a new house. He scanned the local newspapers every day for houses that were for sale and then spent the weekends with the family, looking at the houses that he had shortlisted. Within a month, they decided on a property in Liverpool. It was a three-bedroom house with modern amenities and an asking price that was well within his range. After the usual negotiations, Ranjit purchased the property in Ajoy's name.

Within a few months, the family moved into the new home. It was an exciting time for everyone as they set about organising the new house. They moved most of the old furniture to the new place but Ajoy helped his parents to buy a few appliances, specially for the kitchen. The family settled in admirably well and also had a small house-warming dinner for close friends.

Soon everything returned to normal. Ajoy plodded on with his work and Ranjit started private tuition for school students. Within a few months he built up a large group of students who would usually come for tuition after school hours. Between Ajoy's salary and Ranjit's tuition fees, Lolita found it quite easy to manage the household expenses.

At appropriate moments, they often asked Ajoy to get married.

Since Ajoy had no time for girlfriends, Ranjit even hinted at getting a good girl from India. Ajoy, however, remained steadfastly uninterested, which caused Lolita a lot of grief. She wanted to see Ajoy happily settled with a family of his own.

Thus, life continued without any changes to the routine. There was no ambition and excitement within the household. And yet there was always a pervasive air of happiness within the walls.

The bad news came three years later, a day before Ajoy's birthday.

It was a Saturday evening. As Ranjit and Lolita sat down for dinner, they heard the front door open. They exchanged smiles. Ajoy was back. He had been coming home late for the last month and Lolita suspected that he was seeing someone. Ajoy walked into the dining room and pulled up a chair.

Lolita saw the look of concern in his eyes. 'Is everything all right?' she asked.

Ajoy did not look up for a few moments. When he did, there was a shifty look in his eyes. 'I need to discuss a serious matter with you,' he said at last.

Lolita could detect a slight tremor in his voice.

'I have decided to start up a small business with a friend in Brisbane,' Ajoy said.

'But that is good news indeed,' Ranjit exclaimed.

Ajoy voice dropped. 'It's not all good news, Dad. I need to invest capital in the business. I don't have much in my bank. This house is the only asset that I have.'

His words were met with an uncomfortable silence.

After what seemed to be ages, Lolita spoke up. 'What are you trying to say, Ajoy?'

'I will need to – need to sell this house.' Ajoy's voice was just a whisper.

Ranjit stood up infuriated. 'What? Are you telling me that you want to sell my house? My house? I will not have any of this nonsense.'

'I really have no other option, Dad,' Ajoy replied.

Lolita put a caring hand on Ajoy's shoulder. 'You cannot do such a thing, son. You cannot sell our house.'

Ranjit put his hands on the table and leaned forward. His face was inches away from Ajoy's. 'How dare you?' Ranjit growled. 'How can you even think of selling my house? And after all that we've done for you.'

Ajoy stood up slowly and moved away from the table. When he spoke, there was a slight trace of authority in his voice. 'Dad,' Ajoy said, 'you're forgetting that this is my house. It's in my name.'

Ranjit looked at Ajoy as if he had seen a ghost. He tried to protest but could hardly utter a word. He slumped back into his chair, shaking his head.

Lolita could not control the sudden flood of tears. She took a step towards her son. 'Ajoy,' she pleaded, 'please don't do this to us. We have nowhere to go. We have given you most of our savings. We will be left without a proper roof over our heads.'

Ajoy looked at his mother. There was a hint of compassion in his eyes. 'I am sorry, Ma,' he said. 'I wish I had other alternatives. This business is a one-time opportunity for me. If I don't take this up, I'll never have a future to look forward to. Please try and understand.'

Lolita stood and walked up to Ajoy. 'I am trying to understand, son. But I can't.'

There was a distinct helplessness in her voice that Ranjit had never heard before. 'That's enough, Lolita,' he said harshly. 'I think I know where we stand. We will pack and leave the house within the next two weeks.'

'But wh-where do we go?' Lolita cried out.

Ranjit did not bother to answer. He brushed passed Ajoy and left the room.

The next two weeks were the most harrowing ones that Lolita had ever seen in the household. Ajoy avoided his parents and always came home late. Ranjit, on the other hand, left home early to look for an apartment to rent. Lolita stayed home, alone and depressed. She spent her time talking to friends about her terrible plight. She even inquired if they could get some help from the government or from a charitable organisation. Although she got plenty of sympathy, no one offered to help.

Within a few weeks, Ranjit and Lolita moved out of the house. With the help of a few friends, they moved to a one-room apartment in Emu Plains, a suburb at the foot of the Blue Mountains. Ajoy stayed out of their way during the move and Ranjit refused to speak to his son before leaving the house.

Ranjit's good friend Ramdas Roy came to their help again. He provided Ranjit with a spare room in his house for his daily evening tuition. This suited Ranjit very well since is Ramdas's house was located in the central suburb of Parramatta. To make ends meet, Lolita also accepted a part-time position at a local 7-Eleven owned by an acquaintance. Between the two of them, Ranjit and Lolita earned just enough money to pay the rent, provide for the daily groceries and pay the bills. A friend gave them an old television set and they took a loan from their superannuation fund to buy a little fridge.

On several occasions, Lolita tried calling Ajoy when Ranjit was not home. Her attempts proved futile since her son refused to take her calls. After a month, Ranjit and Lolita were informed by a friend that Ajoy had sold their house and moved to Brisbane.

One evening, Ranjit came back home from his tuition and stopped dead in his tracks as he entered the apartment. On the worn-out table near the door he saw a photograph in a wooden frame. It was a photograph of Ajoy that they had got framed a few years ago.

Ranjit stormed into the minuscule kitchen, where Lolita was preparing dinner. 'Have you put that framed photograph in the living room?' he asked in an infuriated voice.

'Yes,' Lolita replied. She had not expected Ranjit's outburst.

'Why?'

'Because that is the only memory I have of our son.'

Ranjit glared at her. 'I have no son. He died the day he threw us out.'

Lolita looked at him silently. She could feel the tears struggling to get out.

'I want you to take that cursed photograph and put it out of my sight,' Ranjit said.

Lolita hesitated.

'Right now,' Ranjit raised his voice. 'Otherwise I will take it out with the garbage. I do not want to see that bloody photograph again. Never again.'

Lolita stifled a sob and quickly left the kitchen. She did not have dinner that night and retired early.

Next morning, Ranjit walked out to the living room and found that Ajoy's photograph was no longer on the table near the front door. He heaved a sigh of relief. How he hated that photograph and all the memories that came with it.

Months passed by and soon turned into years. Ranjit and Lolita continued with their frugal, unexciting and uneventful lives. Ranjit refused to discuss Ajoy and rejected Lolita's repeated pleas to get in touch with their son. However, unknown to him, Lolita continued to enquire about Ajoy from her friends. She was thrilled to know that Ajoy was doing extremely well in business and was overjoyed when she was told that her son had expanded his operations to India and China. The only news that saddened her was that he had still not married and had given in to the life of a bachelor.

Life chugged along and ten years passed by. Ten years of hard work and penny-pinching survival for Ranjit and Lolita. For a second time in their lives, the unexpected bad tidings came like a bolt from the sky, on a Saturday evening. This time, the bearer of the bad tidings was their friend Ramdas Roy and he had come with some devastating information: Ajoy had died in a fatal accident near Brisbane.

The shattering news destroyed the very souls of Ranjit and Lolita. On hearing the dreadful news, Lolita broke down in mind and spirit and was inconsolable for weeks. But even in her grief, she was shocked to see Ranjit's mental state. He wept silently like a child, for days on end. As the sad news spread through Sydney's Indian community, certain details about Ajoy's life came to light, filtering through friends and acquaintances. The parents came to know about their son's success in business, his enormous wealth, his travels and his lonely life as a bachelor.

Ajoy's body was soon released by the authorities and the parents immediately flew to Brisbane and brought their beloved son back to Sydney. In a quiet ceremony with close friends, on a Friday morning, the body was cremated with the due Hindu rituals at the Springwood Crematorium. It was the saddest day in the lives of Ranjit and Lolita.

Four weeks after Ajoy's death, even before Ranjit and Lolita had had recovered from the shock, they received a letter from a law firm in Brisbane. It was a simple letter stating that, in the absence of a will or other beneficiaries, Australian inheritance laws bequeathed all of Ajoy's wealth to his parents. Ranjit and Lolita became unexpected millionaires in a matter of days and life changed dramatically for them.

Within six months of receiving the letter and after the settlement of the legalities, the couple moved into a modern waterfront mansion in the exclusive suburb of Drummoyne. Together with the house, they also purchased a couple of expensive cars and every contemporary amenity that money could buy.

Once they had settled in the new house, Lolita persuaded Ranjit to organise a celebratory dinner in the memory of their dear departed son. After many hours of discussion, they decided to host the event on Ajoy's birthday.

It was a wonderful occasion. Guests were overwhelmed by the tastefully furnished mansion, the sophisticated cars, the wonderful dinner, the big swimming pool and the exquisitely manicured gardens. But what really took their breath away and brought tears to many eyes was the photograph of Ajoy in an old worn-out wooden frame, displayed proudly on the hand-crafted mantelpiece in front of the main entrance.

Printed in Australia
AUOC02n1458290117
282552AU00002B/10/P

9 781760 412630